KISS THE GIRLS

A gripping serial killer thriller with a dark twist

PETE BRASSETT

Paperback published by The Book Folks

London, 2018

This book is a work of fiction. Names, characters, businesses, organizations, places and events are either the product of the author's imagination or are used fictitiously. Any resemblance to actual persons, living or dead, events or locales is entirely coincidental. The spelling is British English.

ISBN 978-1-7181-9860-9

www.thebookfolks.com

For Strange Girl,
You are beloved.

Prologue

I recall the night I moved to Zanzibar. In fact, I'll never forget it. It was a revelation. It was different. For years I'd wallowed in the suburban security of Strawberry Hill because it seemed like the right thing to do. It wasn't. People thought I was loaded. I wasn't. I was bored. Bored of saying 'Eel Pie Island'. Bored of looking at vacuous couples in Hunter wellies strolling through the park. Bored with television, bored with the mortgage, bored with the bills and bored with working just to stay in the black. I wanted something else, no, needed something else, but I didn't know what. So I relinquished it all. I sold up. Gave myself a kick in the pants. Forced myself to move on. Can't say it was the best decision I ever made, but what the heck. I sold the house and made just enough to pay off the estate agents and the solicitors and stick a grand in the bank. Never liked money. Just as well.

Come the day, the removal men – two blokes with a Luton van – managed to stuff the entire contents of my house into a storage unit fifty feet square. Fifty lousy square feet. I took a long, last look at seven years' worth of faux domesticity, padlocked the door and had an epiphany. I realised society had played a trick on me, the same trick it plays on everyone else. I realised there and then, at that precise moment, that a nice house, filled with nice stuff, was not for my benefit. No. It was to sate the voyeuristic appetites of other homeowners, of friends and family who would come to ogle and enquire if that was Habitat or Heals, Cargo or The Pier, Conran or Starck. I realised that personal well-being didn't come from a fancy showroom and inner peace wasn't available by mail-order. I realised my life, and my income, had been sapped by a desire to surround myself with useless, but aesthetically pleasing, toot. I smiled. I realised I was doing the right thing.

I had a grip packed with just enough clothes to last a week and embarked on a three-month period of bumming around. The experience was truly liberating. I had no responsibilities, no ties, no commitments and no destination. I was free to go wherever I pleased, whenever I pleased. I didn't have to worry about the meter-man or the postman, the dust on the shelves or the overgrown garden. To all intents and purposes, I had disappeared off the face of the earth. I was free. Free as a bird. A bird with no nest to feather. Nowhere to live.

I spent the first few nights sleeping in the office. The couch was no match for a bed but it had its benefits. For example, I had no travelling expenses, I was always there early and I enjoyed full use of all the facilities. The downside was how easily my working day had become extended. I had to move on, so duly took advantage of the friends I had who lived in the city. Only those who lived within walking distance of the office would do. I had become lazy and fearful of public transport. I was back to couches and, sometimes, a spare bedroom, which was good for a while, but then guilt took over and I felt embarrassed, as though I were imposing. Whilst I appreciated, and took advantage of, their hospitality, I was never comfortable. They had their lives and I had mine. I felt like I was walking on eggshells the whole time, trying to do the right thing, you know: fit in, be genial and stay out of the way as much as possible. It was too much of a strain, I kissed them all goodbye.

Consequently, I ensconced myself at the Holiday Inn behind Victoria Station and that's where things really took off. I checked-in, one night at a time, for three nights, then had a chat with the girl on reception. I told her I would be in town indefinitely and asked if she would cut me a deal. She did. I was in, at a discounted rate that worked out less than renting a flat. I became a resident and I felt like a rock star. It was nothing short of brilliant, while it lasted. I could roll in whenever I liked, with whomever I liked. Room service furnished me with hot meals and cold beer. Maid service took care of my laundry and changed the bed linen on a daily basis and I got my messages without having to ask for them. If I needed postage stamps, cash or a taxi, all I had to do was ask. But, like most things in life, it had to end. It's just a shame it was sooner rather than later.

After nearly two months of being treated like royalty, money became tight. I needed somewhere to live, somewhere more permanent. Somewhere cheap, cheerful and quick. Two out of three, I thought at the time, wasn't bad. I got cheap and quick.

To my surprise, whilst I'd been living the life of Reilly, the cost of renting a flat in town had soared. When I discovered the going rate I almost died. I should have, a funeral would have been cheaper. £400.00 a week. Over a grand a month! Minimum! That wasn't just ridiculous, that was extortion. Pure extortion by the property mongers of Old London Town. I felt a passionate empathy with the teachers, the nurses and the librarians. The firefighters, the ambulance service and the care-workers. How on earth did they cope? On their wages? Okay, I could look for something cheaper, like renting a room rather than a whole flat, but I'd been there before and wasn't about to go back. Never go back.

I was ravaged by the three D's: despair; despondency and desperation; made worse by the fact that the whole of London was celebrating the election of a new Prime Minister. A magician who had hood-winked the nation by putting a red cover on the Conservative manifesto. Blair and his woodentops danced like dads at a school disco to 'Things can only get better'. I thought, 'No. No they can't'.

The imminent downturn in the country's equilibrium was not something I could concern myself with. I had to prioritise, put myself first. I set about locating a large cardboard box, somewhere near Vauxhall station, with hot and cold running air, when, through a friend of a friend, I heard of a place.

'Near Tower Bridge,' they said. 'Great views up-river,' they said. 'Half hour walk to Waterloo.' they said. 'Shut up! I'll take it!' I said, 'Sounds too good to be true!' Well, it was, and it wasn't.

I went to see the owner in the pub where she worked. It was sometime late November, it was after seven and it was dark. From the rain-soaked gloom of the street, the pub looked welcoming and warm. It was saying: 'Come, come tarry a while and have your fill.' It read my mind, I was in the mood for a pint, almost gagging, until I walked in, that is. The place fell silent as I closed the door behind me. It was populated with gangsters, I mean, real South London gangsters. You can tell. If you've been around, believe me, you can tell.

'Aliens have landed,' yelled one smartarse from the corner. All eyes were on me as I approached the bar.

'Alright… Tracy around?' I asked.

'Who's asking?' replied the barman.

'Just tell 'er, Dan's 'ere,' I said, trying to sound as hard as possible.

Two minutes later, Tracy appeared and the pub returned to normal. If I knew Trace, I was alright. She filled me in on the flat while I supped a free pint of Fosters: secure entryphone system; forty-foot, open-plan lounge/diner with river views; washing-machine; oven/hob/grill, microwave, bathroom with power shower; separate toilet and two bedrooms. £500.00 a month, all in. No bills and no questions asked. Enough said, know what I mean?

I'd landed on my feet, couldn't believe my luck. £500? Result. She'd obviously picked up one of those trendy new apartments round the corner on Shad Thames and was letting it out. Why so cheap? Some questions, you just don't ask. I took out my chequebook.

'Two months do ya?' I asked

'You're 'aving a laugh,' she said, 'one month'll do, Dan, one month. You've got an honest face.'

I smirked. Seemed like she was flirting with me.

'Looks can be deceptive,' I said and handed her the cheque. 'So, when could I move in…'

'Got the motor outside, I'll run ya there now, if ya want. You can move in tonight.'

'Perfect. Trace, Bleedin' perfect!'

* * *

I downed my pint, jumped in the car and off we went. We travelled east along Jamaica Road and my confidence ebbed as Tower Bridge faded in the wing-mirror and, along with it, any dream I had of a fancy apartment. Canary Wharf grew bigger and bigger. I had no idea where I was, where I was headed or if I'd ever get back. We passed the Rotherhithe Tunnel and I remember thinking: oh fuck, this is it, tonight I am going to die.

We turned off Lower Road, without slowing, and I was dragged into the bowels of a council estate. Why I was filled with trepidation, I do not know. To this day, I do not know. I was a tearaway as a kid but no worse than the others on the street. I've slept on benches in Paris, beaches in Marbella and ATM lobbies in New York City. I've lived the high life in a Milanese penthouse and shared a squat with certifiable nutcases in Hackney, so the trepidation I experienced was irrational. Stupid and irrational. With the benefit of hindsight, I can only put it down to age, that and the reputation the area had. 'Downtown', as it was known, was a haven for the unemployed and unemployable, immigrants and social misfits. An area where GBH, ABH and TDA constituted a good night out.

We stopped at the foot of a tower block. We had arrived. Zanzibar House. The main door had an entryphone, she hadn't lied about that. There were two lifts, one for the odd-numbered floors, and one for the even. They were all odd to me. We got in the 'even' lift and I was advised, if it was ever out of service, to take the other one and walk down a flight. I was blinded by the logic. The lift had an interesting aroma, a mixture of tobacco, sweat and urine. The door clunked shut and elevated us skywards. I exhaled when we reached the fourteenth floor. Any longer and I would have turned blue.

The door to the flat was solid, obviously reinforced and it had three locks. I followed Tracey into the hallway and it was then I realised she was offering me Del-Boy's flat. It was amazing. Truly amazing.

'I'll tell ya now, it's alright, bit basic, but then I'm not much of a 'omebird, me,' she said.

She wasn't kidding. The hallway was covered in three types of wallpaper, none of which matched the carpet, some of which peeled lazily from the wall. The lounge was adequately furnished, most of it MFI, circa 1972. A pack of cheap, china poodles stared menacingly from the shelves on the wall. A donkey that looked as if it had walked from the Costa del Sol stood forlornly on the mantlepiece. The bathroom walls had a unique mix of paper and bare plaster and there was no bulb in the spare room. Apart from that, everything was as she'd said, just different to what I'd imagined. Just different. Most importantly though, it was clean. It was warm and clean.

She tossed me the keys, pointed out a Tesco from the window and left, a little too quickly for my liking. I was alone, alone and thankful that I'd eaten. Thankful that I had three cans of Miller in my bag and extremely bloody relieved to find a full packet of fags in my pocket.

I checked out the flat, did the usual things, you know: opened all the cupboards, sniffed the sheets to check they were clean and flicked the switches on and off. I scrutinised the plates for signs of crusty debris, checked the taps functioned as they should and then locked myself in. I was a tenant in a not-quite-legal sublet, but it was my pad. My 'bachelor-pad', as Trace put it. I was warming to it, especially the view. It compensated for everything else.

I spent the rest of the evening hanging out of the window, drinking beer and smoking Marlboro Lights. The astounding view looked straight up river: Tower Bridge; The Lloyds Building; St. Paul's Cathedral; The Shell Centre; NatWest Tower; CentrePoint; The Post Office Tower. They sparkled and shone in the night, like the blue lights on the squad cars that called incessantly at the estate.

I listened to the shouting and the screaming, the torrents of abuse and the threats of violence that came from the denizens of the Zanzibar Estate. It was astounding how clear everything was from fourteen floors up. I've been to Zanzibar. It was nothing like Zanzibar. Nothing like it.

Sleep did not come easy that night. Strange noises and the howling wind conjured up images of unemployed axe-men beating a path to my door. I asked God to wake me in the morning. In fact I pleaded with Him to make sure I woke up, full stop. I also asked Him to return the gift of sanity to the voting public, as quickly as possible.

As luck would have it, I did wake up, usual time as it happens, around six. I headed straight for the shower and groaned as a feeble flow of pressure-less water spurted onto my back. At least it was warm.

It was still dark when I left and for that, I was thankful. I felt safe and secure, the dark was now my ally. With no tube nearby, I walked a course that paralleled the river and, as promised, I was at Waterloo inside a half an hour. The Waterloo in desperate need of regeneration. What those tourists must think when they arrive on the Eurostar is beyond me.

I passed the 'homeless' girl with the dog. She was sitting on the pavement outside McDonald's, begging for change. I knew her, by sight, and she didn't cut any ice with me. She lived in a council flat on Bayliss Road and feigned homelessness to supplement her dole.

Tattoo man tried in vain to walk a straight line towards me, roll-up in one hand, can of Special Brew in the other, his combat fatigues weary from years of urban warfare. To this day I cannot fathom what possessed him to get his entire face tattooed with an indigo-coloured spider's web. I doubt he even knew it was there.

As I turned the corner into Morley Street I was greeted by the familiar site of freshly laid faeces scattered across the pavement. This riled me because, in all my time there, I never once saw a stray dog. The perpetrators were always attached to a leash when they emptied their bowels, so the way I see it, it was the owners' responsibility to clean it up, but did they? No, course not. They simply didn't care. They were simply too selfish to care.

Anyway, the day passed without event and the time came to make my way back to hell. I couldn't be bothered with the walk, so that night I rode the bus, a P13. It dropped me right outside the estate exactly twelve minutes later. Now that's what I call commuting.

Enveloped by the night, I strode confidently through the grounds towards Zanzibar. Small gangs of post-pubescent kids hung around the benches and talked amongst themselves. They were loud but they were harmless and they all dressed the same. The boys wore fake Tommy jackets, big training shoes that wouldn't lace up and ridiculous jeans with the crotch by their knees. Their hair was short and caked in too much gel. The girls wore ski-pants and pony-tails, stilettos and ankle bracelets, and not much up top. Their faces were pale and each clutched a pack of Embassy No.1 to their bosom, nipples erect as they shivered in the cold.

Judging by their behaviour, I guessed the average age for cherry-picking in the neighbourhood was fourteen or fifteen, and it seemed to be an al fresco affair, whatever the weather.

I noticed the cars parked in the approach road for the first time. I mean, really noticed them. It stunned me. They were all relatively new and rather incongruous. I counted a Cherokee, an Audi TT, a Nissan Micra, a Polo, an Espace and a Discovery to name but a few, but the most noticeable thing about them was the damage. There was none. No bent aerials, no scratched paintwork and no broken windows. There seemed to be some kind of code of respect within the estate and, for whatever reason that may have been, I believed it to be good.

I hit the fourteenth floor and met a neighbour, the guy who lived opposite. He was younger than me, about twenty-eight I guess, and keen to introduce himself. Keen to mingle with the denizens of this vertical village. He worked in the City, dressed like Beau Brummel and thought the estate epitomised sixties cool. Yeah baby! Yeah, right.

As it happens, he wasn't alone. In the weeks that followed I met a few other 'arty' types who shared his outlook. There were the mandatory students, a photographer, two painters and, surprisingly, a handful of aspiring writers, all of whom mingled freely with the pensioners, the single mums and the Nigerian doctors who promised to 'clear your life of ailments and solve problems with business or marriage'.

Whatever they were, the one thing they had in common, was that they were all polite. They'd all say hello, or stop and chat, and that made a difference. Okay, I admit some of them probably robbed a bank or two, or indulged in the odd bit of knee-capping, but that was their business and I didn't want to know about it.

About a month passed and I was feeling settled, comfortable, you know? Yet in all that time there was still one person I hadn't met, my immediate neighbour, the guy next door. I got back one night, late it was, about eleven, and Sod's law, I thought about it and there he was, struggling with a bin sack. Not surprising really, considering his age. I offered to help and took it down to the refuse area. It was heavy and it smelled. When I returned, he was waiting, full of gratitude.

He must've been about eighty odd, maybe a bit older, and he stooped slightly. His hair was thin, white and thin, and he wore half-rim specs on the bridge of his nose. A dead roll-up hung from his bottom lip and, apart from his tartan slippers, I'd say he was still in his de-mob suit.

I smiled politely when I saw him, and couldn't help but notice the stains on his jacket, which also ran the length of his pants. 'Poor bugger,' I thought, 'hope I don't end up like you'.

'Thanks son,' he croaked, his voice tarnished with war and nicotine, 'appreciate it. Not many like you round here, bleedin' tossers, the lot of them, wouldn't piss on ya if you was on fire.'

'Yeah, right, no sweat. Look, if you need anything, just shout, okay, I'm right next door.'

'You're a good sort, lad. Come and have a drink, glass of sherry, for taking the rubbish, be grateful for the company.'

'Well, I'd like to, but…'

'Alright! Suit yourself!' he moaned, 'do what ya bleedin' well…'

'Okay! Okay, great, come on granddad, let's have that sherry, I could do with a drink. I'm Dan.'

'More like it, son. I'm Stan. Stan, the fuckin' man.'

* * *

I was impressed. Stan's flat was a damned site nicer than mine, by which I mean it had wallpaper that stayed up. It was immaculate. For an old-timer on welfare, he seemed to be doing okay. I learned very quickly he was a local, almost, and had moved to Zanzibar when they knocked his house down, near the Old Kent Road. He'd lived, I assumed, on his own ever since. He never mentioned a wife and I wasn't going to bring it up. Not the kind of question you just blurt out. Especially to an octogenarian.

Unlike my place, the wallpaper matched the carpet, the table seated four but was set for one and there were no tacky artifacts to be seen. It was tasteful in a 'nice-grandparent' sort of way. Homely, even. There were a few black and white photos of him in service uniform atop the sideboard and a clutch of medals stood proudly on display in a glass cabinet.

'Make yourself comfy, boy, I'll get that sherry,' he said. 'Emva Cream or Amon'illado?'

'Whatever you're having,' I said. 'Don't mind.'

'Glass of port then. Can't stand sherry, only keep it for the bleedin' old girl downstairs. Nosy cow.'

'How's that?'

'Well, keeps comin' in, don't she, keeps comin' in to see if I'm alright. If I'm alright, what she's really doin' is sticking her big bloody nose in to see what I've done with the place.'

'What do you mean?'

'I'm a decorator, ain't I? Kind of. I like to decorate. Done the bedroom twice last year.'

'Twice…! That's a bit bloody keen, I mean…'

'It's what I do, alright! It's what I bleedin' well do. Like to keep meself busy.'

'Right. Nice papering,' I said, trying to change the subject.

'Eh?'

'Nice papering. I always get bubbles.'

'Well now, that's cos you ain't doin' it right,' he said. 'You're rushin' it. Probably using all that modern crap as well.'

'Ay? Modern…'

'Leave it. son, next time. Trade secret, ain't it?'

'Yeah, okay. Look I gotta get back, early start, ya know?'

'S'alright, boy. Glad to see ya got some work ethics, not like the other good for…'

'Thanks for the drink.'

'Tell ya what, drop in tomorrow. I'll tell ya a fing or two, I will.'

'I'll do that. What time?'

'Time? How do I know what time? Whenever you bleedin' well get 'ere…'

* * *

I left, and not before time. Cantankerous, belligerent, and possibly bigoted, were descriptions that filled my head. I couldn't make up my mind about him. On the one hand I thought, silly old git, I'll never see him again, on the other, I thought, poor sod, he's on his own, maybe he's like that because he's lonely. Either way, my opinion seemed too trivial to waste time thinking about it. I went to bed.

The next day was miserable, it rained incessantly, no thunder or lightning, just a continual downpour. The city seemed grey and bleak. Well, greyer and bleaker than normal. I walked to work and got completely drenched. It was the start of an uneventful day which dragged on for an age. By the time I got back to Zanzibar the rain had stopped and the natives were restless.

Dressed in hooded tops and baseball caps, the lads walked in circles in a manner that suggested one leg was shorter than the other. Their dialect was a poor man's Patwa, surprising as they were all Caucasian and probably couldn't even point to Jamaica on a map. Their speech was punctuated with wildly exaggerated arm movements, not unlike the badass rappers who seemed to have taken over Top of the Pops.

In contrast, the girls, who were probably referred to as 'bitches', sat huddled together, like Siamese septuplets. They chewed gum and drew heavily on their fags. Occasionally, they'd smile coyly at one of the lads and mutter 'Alright?'. It was obviously a mating ritual of sorts, primeval and basic, if not saddeningly crude. I wondered if they'd ever grow up, maybe progress to using the Queen's English or even realise that IQ wasn't something you did in the supermarket. I walked on by and felt my age, I was obviously becoming an 'old fart' ahead of time.

I remembered the promise I'd made to Stan but the prospect of spending a couple of hours in his company filled me with dread. I simply wasn't in the mood. I tried opening the door as quietly as possible but with more keys than a jail warden the noise was unavoidable. I turned around and there he was, waiting. I knew there was no escape. Before he could speak, I told him to wait while I dumped my bag and coat. In the few seconds I had, I snatched another pack of Marlboro Lights and a four-pack of Miller from the fridge. I had an unreasonable preconception that the only refreshment he would offer would be port, sherry or a small can of Mackeson. I felt grubby and wanted to wash, but I daren't keep him waiting. I ventured out again.

'Alright son?' he said. 'Had yer dinner? Got a couple of kippers left, they're still warm.'

'Thanks Stan, I've eaten. Got a Kentucky on the way,' I replied, lying through my front teeth. I was famished.

'Come on, got something to show ya.'

I followed him in and paused by the bathroom. The door was locked.

'Stan, mind if I wash my hands, I feel a bit…'

'Not there! Come in here, use the sink.'

We walked to the kitchen.

'Jesus, Stan! You sure those kippers were alright, it stinks in here!'

'Nuffin' wrong with the kippers, lad. I've been making glue, that's all. I'll open the window.'

'Making…?'

* * *

The kitchen was a mess, the antithesis of the showflat I'd seen the night before. The sink was full of scummy water, two pan handles poked through the surface like they were gasping for air. The drainer was covered in soiled Tupperware boxes, ketchup stains, a dirty plate and a rusty meat cleaver. The work-top was the same. Stinking pieces of meat mingled with bone-chippings and something resembling chicken skin. The place was like an abattoir.

I deferred the hand-washing, took a seat on his sofa and cracked open a can of Miller. It went down remarkably quickly.

'Ere, take a look at this,' he said, and shoved a paint kettle in my face. It was filled with a glutinous liquid, the likes and colour of which, I'd never seen before. It stank.

'Know what that is?' he said with a grin. 'Animal glue.'

'What? Animal… what the fuck are you talking…'

'Best glue you'll ever get. But you won't get it in any bleedin' B & Q, I'll tell ya that for nuffin'.'

'I believe you, but what… I mean… why? What's it for?'

'In the old days see, before Mr Bleedin' Polywhatsit started making all that crap, animal glue is what we used. In the trade. That's where I learned it, as a carpenter. Animal glue, see, stick anything it will – for good. Ya soak it for a bit in lime, boil down the bones and all the other crap, add a bit of glycerine, and Bob's your uncle. Let it set, stick it in the fridge and cut off bits when ya need it.'

'Right, I…'

'Then ya just warm it up, with a bit of water like, and off ya go.'

'Oh, right,' I said, not sure if I was surprised, bewildered or impressed. 'Well, you learn something new every day. So, where d'you get the stuff from then, to make it? The bones and stuff?'

'Whatcha mean? I don't kill nothing… get it down the butchers, don't I, where else would I…'

'Yeah, course. So, you make this up every time you're gonna do a bit of decorating then?'

'S'right. Water it down for the papering, bit thicker for the other stuff, cupboards like, know what I mean?'

'Yeah, yeah, I'm with you.'

'Right, I'll put this away. 'Ere, get us a drink, boy, on the side there, large port. Glasses in the cupboard.'

'Alright, no trouble.'

I began to relax, old Stan was alright and I'd learned something too. I wasn't fooling myself though, I knew the Miller was helping me through. I uncorked the port and opened the cupboard to get a glass.

The first thing I saw was another Tupperware box, a small one, about five inches square, no lid. It was about half full of jewellery, women's jewellery. Rings, brooches and necklaces, some gold, some silver. I assumed they belonged to his wife. Ex-wife. Deceased wife. He caught me looking at it when he returned.

'Oi! Whatcha doin' in there?'

'Nothing! Just getting a glass, saw this, that's all. Your wife's, eh?'

'Wife? Oh, yeah, wife. That's right.'

'You oughtta keep this lot somewhere safe, Stan. Worth a bob or two, by the looks of it.'

'Yeah, yeah, but I need it, for paper and stuff.'

'Paper? I'm not with you.'

'Decorating. I'm a bleedin' pensioner, ain't I? How'd ya think I pay for all this? Scotch bleedin' mist?'

'You sell it?'

'Nah, pawn it, when I have to. Don't give me that bleedin' look mate, it's the only pleasure I got in life these days.'

'I ain't looking at you like nothing, Stan. I understand. It's alright by me.'

'Well. Some people, you know what they're…'

'I know, and I ain't one of 'em. Still, better the jewellery than the medals, eh? I mean, that's personal, right?'

'Right you are, lad, but I ain't so proud that I wouldn't sell 'em. Don't mean nothing to me. Did my bit and that's that.'

'How d'ya mean?'

'War. Killing people, ain't right. Specially when you're the one that's gotta fix 'em up.'

'So you were Medical Corps, then?'

'Unofficially. Did what we had to in them days. Just helped out, learned stuff as I went along.'

'Well, you must've been good at it, I mean, you've got the medals. Where'd you fight?'

'Eighth Army mainly, Bombardier Wilkins, that was me. Did North Africa, El Alamein…'

'Ah! One of Monty's lot, a Desert Rat!'

'No son, not bleedin' Monty. Gatehouse. 10th Armoured. Bleedin' fiasco that was. Had us running round in circles, he did.'

'So what are they for then, the medals? What do they mean?'

'That one, that's the Thirty-Nine/ Forty-Five Star, that's the France and Germany Star and that one, in the middle, that's the Africa Star, that is, with the Eighth Army Clasp.'

'Impressive, Stan. We owe you, all of us, that's the way I see it, anyway.'

'Thanks lad. People these days got short memories. Short memories and no bleedin' respect. Now, nuff said. You alright with that beer there?'

'Yeah, fine. Here's your port. Cheers. Anyway, you were saying, glue. What's it for?'

'Bog. That's why you can't go in there. Prepping it, ain't I.'

A knock at the door interrupted our conversation. It wasn't an apologetic knock, but a severe, deliberate, bam, bam, bam. Someone was after Stan. That struck me as odd for three reasons. One: Stan lived alone and from what I'd gathered, he didn't have any friends. Two: It was getting on, as I recall, it was gone seven. And three: Stan was in no hurry to answer it.

'Who the bleedin' hell is that?' he said, his voice was deliberately low, like he didn't want to be found. 'Why don't they sod off and leave me alone! Don't they know what time it is?'

'I'll get it if you like,' I said. 'Just in case, you know?'

'Yeah, you get it, and tell 'em I'm in bed! Bloody cheek they got.'

* * *

I opened the door mid-way through a second chorus on the letter-box. A plain but attractive woman, about forty-ish, stood on the doorstep. She had her hair tied back in a no-nonsense fashion, clutched a shoulder bag and wore flat shoes. From beneath her top-coat, what looked like a nurse's uniform gripped her wine-glass calves.

'And you are?' she asked. Her inquisitive manner was blunt and her tone, to the point, but it didn't come across as rude. The lilting Galway accent cushioned the severity of her question.

'Dan,' I replied. 'You?'

'Don't give me none of your nonsense, mister. Where's Stan? Stanley Wilkins!' she hollered, 'If you don't come out here right this minute there'll be hell to pay, you mark my words!'

I smiled, somewhat infected by her forceful manner, but I knew it was a front. Underneath it all, I had the feeling she was as gentle as a lamb. She caught me smiling and winked back, as if to say: 'watch this, the silly old fool needs a lesson, so he does'.

Stan ambled to the door and cowered behind me.

'You're a blinkin' fool, Stanley Wilkins,' she continued. 'I'm here for your benefit, not mine! You should open the door when I call. Lord knows, I've enough to do as it is.'

'Alright, alright,' said Stan. 'Been busy, ain't I.'

'Busy, my…'

'Look, I best leave you to it,' I said. 'I've got stuff to do.'

'Grand! It's just a check-up and a few exercises, that's the only reason I call, though Lord knows why I'm doing it now, just look at the time. Slave to myself, so I am.'

'You better come in,' said Stan, 'I'll stick the kettle on.'

She unbuttoned her coat to reveal a starched, white uniform bound tightly around an incredibly small waist. Actually, it probably just seemed small because of her petite frame and child-bearing hips, but I rather hoped I'd meet her again. I assumed she was single because she didn't wear a ring, but it wasn't the time, nor the place, for dating games.

'I'll get out your way,' I said. 'If you need anything, I'm just next door.'

Her eyes glinted mischievously.

'Thanks,' she said, smiling. 'Mary's the name, maybe see you again?'

* * *

Me and an older woman? Me and a nurse? Nah. Anyway, after that, I didn't see Stan for three weeks. Apart from the occasional toilet flush, which I heard through the walls, there was no sign of life in his flat. I admit, I was in the habit of leaving at dawn and returning after eight, so I had little opportunity to gauge the extent of his activities, but even so.

At first, I was glad, in a selfish way. A part of me could live quite happily without the ramblings of a bitter, old man bordering on senility, but then I became concerned. Concerned because I knew him, because he was old and because I'd been raised to respect my elders, whatever their disposition. Each evening I knocked on his door, I knocked and I shouted through the letter-box, but there was no response. I was on the verge of calling the police, fearful he had fallen or had a cardiac, when out of the blue, just like that, he knocked on my door. It was a Tuesday night. I remember that because every Monday I used to grab a take-away, on account of drinking too much beer at lunchtime, and every Tuesday I'd hit Tesco to stock up on Tropicana and two days' worth of monosodium glutamate. I'd just shoved a Finest Lamb Shank with Ratatouille in the oven when there was a knock at the door. He took me by surprise.

'Alright lad? Now, come and 'ave a look at this. Finished the bog, ain't I.'

'Stan! Where the fuck have you been? I've been…'

'Told ya, I been busy, ain't I. Now, get your skates on, ain't got all day.'

He didn't have all day and I had roughly half an hour or my shank would be shafted. I grabbed a Miller from the fridge and followed him round to his place.

'Go on,' he said, 'just you take a look at that.'

He'd surpassed himself. The bathroom wasn't exactly to my tastes, but I could appreciate workmanship when I saw it. The enamelled tub and porcelain fixtures were identical to mine, but the decor was a million miles away. I had peeling paper and bare plaster, he had a 'tranquil haven of serenity'. The walls were a muted, daffodil-yellow with a pastel-green trim embossed with a palm tree motif. I inspected them closely and was damned if I could find a join. He'd even papered around the cupboard on the wall, but you wouldn't have known it. On the floor, an island of a bathmat floated on a sea of powder-blue linoleum tiles.

I was impressed, not simply by the quality of his work but, more importantly, because it must have taken the old boy an absolute age to do it. I thought, if I'm capable of that at seventy, then something's wrong, because I'm totally incapable now.

'So, whatcha think?' asked Stan. It was the first time I'd seen him smile. He was justifiably proud of his achievement and I wasn't going to pour water on his fire.

'Stan,' I said, 'it's brilliant! I don't know how you do it, but you've got a talent there, no doubt about it.'

'Glad ya like it. Now come on, I got some beer in and I've made us some sarnies. I got beef spread and Dairylea, you alright with that?'

I couldn't refuse, could I? How could I? I nipped back to the flat, kissed my shank goodbye, and returned to Stan's. He'd set the table for two, placemats and everything. A mound of Mother's Pride sandwiches, cut into quarters, sat centre-stage, and a four-pack of cheap lager sat next to a bottle of port.

Bless his cotton socks, I knew he wasn't the cranky, old sod I'd first met and was glad to be taken into his confidence. I sat down and actually looked forward to what remained of the evening, his stories, some idle banter and the sealing of a friendship. The feeling was reciprocated, or at least, that's how it seemed. I got the impression he was glad of the company, glad to have someone he could talk with, educate maybe, and possibly, even laugh. He was opening up and I felt privileged to be there for the unveiling.

I picked up a sarnie and asked about his family, I figured, if he thought I was being intrusive, he'd tell me to bugger off. He didn't.

'Family? Got none, son. Nah, no family, just me.'

'Shame,' I said. 'They passed on? Moved away?'

'Nah, never had no-one else, only child.'

'What about the in-laws, the wife's family?'

'Wife? Getoutofit! Bleedin' wives. No. Never married, not me.'

'Eh? But I thought that jewellery, in the cupboard, you said it was…'

'Mother's. Old girl's stuff.'

'Oh, sorry, I just thought…'

'No matter. 'Ere, have a spread this time,' he said, pushing the plate of sandwiches towards me. 'Shippam's that is. You'll like it. As for women, forget 'em. Take my advice son, you're better off without 'em. You steppin' out or you single? 'Ere, you ain't one of those, one of those whatsits, queer types?'

'Ha! No Stan, I ain't one of those, I'm single. Just split with a bird actually, didn't work out.'

'Don't surprise me, you stay clear of 'em, I'm telling ya, you're better off on your own. You'll only get hurt.'

I was surprised. It was obviously a sore point with him, I didn't want to push my luck, but I wanted to know more. Had he been spurned, or jilted even? I got in the same boat and changed my tact.

'I know what you mean, Stan, but you have to admit, there a few gooduns about.'

'Maybe, son, maybe. But they'll screw you in the end.'

'So tell me, what happened when you got back after your discharge, like?'

'Went home didn't I?'

'Home? Where was that?'

'Old Kent Road and what a mess that was. Gerry done us good, make no mistake. Blimey, what a mess.'

'Must've been quite a homecoming, though, your parents must've been proud.'

'They weren't there, well, just the old girl, and some bleedin' fancy-man.'

'What about your dad? Where was he?'

'Dead. Trampled to death, he was. Bethnal Green, apparently.'

'Sorry mate, trampled?'

'S'right. In the rush to get underground. Stampede it was, during a raid. Well they said it was a raid. Coupla hundred bought it, and not a bomb in sight.'

'Bloody hell! That's tragic. Tragic. But you, you got back home, Old Kent Road, and…'

'And there was me mum, with some geezer who was too bloody queer to fight like the rest of us. Twenty-two I was. Twenty-two. Made me mad, I can tell ya.'

'Hold up, what do you mean, too queer to fight?'

'Bleedin' conchie, weren't he.'

'Conchie?'

'Conscientious Objector.'

'You didn't like 'em then?'

'No one did, son. No one. I mean, none of us wanted to fight, see, but we did. We did it cos we had to, we did it cos we didn't want no bleedin' Nazis telling us what to do. Likes of him let us to do their dirty work for 'em while they stayed home, all warm and cosy, like.'

'So, this bloke, this conchie, he sort of helped out then, did he?'

'Ya might say that. Him and half of Southwark. See, things was tight then, son, we had rationing. Survived on pennies, we did. I'll tell ya something else too, we didn't have no beef spread in them days, bread and dripping is what we had, and thankful for it. Even so, she didn't have to do that.'

'Do what? I'm not with you, Stan.'

'Take men in.'

'Lodgers?'

'Gawd almighty, not bleedin' lodgers! Blimey, you thick or something? Men. She offered her services.'

'Wha…? You mean she…?'

'That's exactly what I mean. Just so she could swan round like the Queen of bleedin' Sheba and look better than the rest of us. Slag.'

'Stan, that is your mum you're talking about.'

'Listen, son, every slag has a mother, and most of 'em end up being mothers themselves. I ain't being disrespectful, that's what she was and that's all there is to it.'

'Fair enough, mate. Fair enough. So, you moved here when she passed away then? Is that right?'

'Passed away? Went away more like. Did a flit with some geezer and just disappeared she did, without a trace.'

'What? How'd you… didn't the police try looking for her?'

'Everyone did. Last we knew she was in Margate but can't say for sure. Dunno where she went. I stuck around in the old place, nearly twenty years, but things changed. That's when I come here. New start, like.'

* * *

Bingo! There it was, the reason why Stan had such volatile opinions on the fairer sex. The reason why he'd remained single all his life: his mother. I'm no psychologist, but I was certain he was a textbook case. It was sad, not because she'd become a wanton hussy, but because her lifestyle had had such a damaging effect on Stan.

I polished off another sandwich and pondered, momentarily, as to what he could have been. I mean, what he could have made of himself. Teacher? Civil Servant? Family man, even. I had a hunch that, given different circumstances, he would have made somebody a great father, and a great husband. It was a shame.

'Last one, son. Go on, you 'ave it,' said Stan, pointing at the Dairylea.

'No thanks, really, I'm full,' I said. 'You have it. Tell you what though, wouldn't mind a glass of port.'

'Help yerself, ya know where the glasses are.'

'Cheers. I'll bring you a bottle tomorrow, my treat.'

* * *

I liked Stan. There was more to him than met the eye, and if it hadn't been so late, I'd have stayed for hours, but there was always tomorrow.

I took a glass from the cupboard and as I turned back, I noticed a brown, shoulder bag on the sofa, half hidden by a cushion. It was a lady's bag and it looked familiar.

'Here, Stan,' I said, holding it aloft, 'ain't this the nurse's bag?'

'Eh? Whassat?'

'The bag, looks like the one your nurse was carrying.'

'Is it? Stupid cow, must've forgotten it. See what I mean about women? Forget their bleedin' heads if they weren't screwed on.'

'Yeah, maybe, but that's gotta be, what, couple of weeks ago now, and she ain't called back?'

'Well, she obviously don't need it, does she?'

I thought it odd. Very odd. In my experience I had learned that women and bags go together. They're like ham and eggs or stew and dumplings. They're inseparable. They carry their lives in their bags and without them they're helpless. I just couldn't see how she could live without it, unless, it was just work stuff, ointments and the like, just for Stan.

I put down the glass, sat on the edge of the sofa, and took a look inside. Stan was oblivious to my actions, he was sipping his port and humming to himself. I wanted the bag to be full of medical notes, bandages and rubs. I was horribly wrong, and it made me feel very uncomfortable. Staring back at me was her driving licence: Mary O'Shaughnessy, 43 Alma Grove, Bermondsey. There was an NHS identity card, a cheque book, credit card wallet, a couple of envelopes, a lipstick and a set of house-keys.

'Stan,' I said. 'Stan, something ain't right. All her stuff's here, everything. Something must've…'

There was a knock at the door. It stopped me mid-sentence. Stan carried on humming while I answered it. I hoped it was Mary, come to claim her belongings, but I was wrong again.

Two men and a woman stood outside. They were nothing special to look at, very ordinary in fact. One man, about five-seven with a grubby mac over a cheap-looking suit, the other, old. The woman looked out of place. She was shorter, say five-four, with short, dark hair and piercing green eyes. She had a heart-shaped face and sharp, chiselled features. By no means unattractive. She smiled as the younger of the men pulled a card from his pocket and held it to my face.

'D.I. Hanlon,' he said. 'Walworth C.I.D. This is D.C. Porter, retired, and Detective Sergeant Scott. We're looking for Stanley Wilkins. He in?'

As he spoke, two uniformed officers stepped from the lift and hovered in the background.

'Yeah, yeah, he's inside,' I said. 'What's up? What's he done? Is it serious?'

'You'll find out soon enough, sir. Can we come in? Thanks. Oh and, er, don't go far, we might need to ask you some questions.'

I stepped aside and watched them walk down the hall to the dining room. Stan had his back to us. He didn't look round, he just sat there and sipped his port till the old fellow spoke.

* * *

'Stanley Wilkins?'

'That you, Plod? Blimey! After all these years, if it ain't Constable Porter! Don't you ever give up?'

'Not me, Stanley, you know what they say, slowly, slowly, catchy monkey. Got a few questions but you'll have to come with us I'm afraid…'

'Come with you? Not on your bleedin' Nellie.'

'I'm sorry Mr Wilkins, but if you don't…'

'Listen, Plod, I told ya, I ain't goin' down no nick. You got something to say, say it, otherwise, keep your trap shut.'

'I have to warn you Wilkins, if you…'

He was cut short by the commotion at the front door.

Chapter One

The pillar box stood proud, defiantly erect like a periscope in a sea of rubble. The postman crouched on his haunches and emptied the mail into his sack. He was dressed in full GPO uniform, his cap rested at a jaunty angle on the back of his head. He was happy with his lot and, like every other man, woman and child, was happy the war was over. As far as they were concerned, it was business as usual.

He shut the box and watched as yet another de-mobbed Tommy clambered over the bricks and mortar towards him. He whistled 'Roll me over, in the clover', clutched a copy of the Daily Express in one hand and a brown, paper parcel in the other.

It was a little after three o'clock on the tenth of February, 1946 and Stanley Wilkins was back from the war.

'Welcome home mate!' yelled the postman.

'Ta!' replied Stan. 'Blimey, this place has changed a bit, ain't it?'

'Changed ain't the word, you try delivering these when there ain't no letter-box!'

'Ha, ha! 'Ere, Twenty-Two still standing?'

'Your lucky day, mate, Twenty-Two and Twenty-Four're the only ones left. Over there, see? By the milk float.'

'Right you are, thanks mate.'

'Be lucky!'

* * *

The house hadn't changed, it was just as Stan remembered it, but without the adjoining terraces it looked more regal. Posh, like an expensive, detached residence. He stood on the front step, adjusted his hat and stood tall, shoulders back. He was keen to see his family and eager for them to see the man he'd become. Mentally, the war had aged him, he had matured. He was wiser than his years and more than capable of handling anything civvy street could throw at him. Nervously, he rapped the door, took a pace back and waited. Gladys Wilkins, the mother he hadn't seen for five years and seven months, opened the door. He found it hard not to grin. She looked stunning. At thirty-nine she was still a looker, enhanced by the fact that she was dressed, rather incongruously, in a black evening gown.

'Allo, Ma!' he said, unsure if he should embrace her or shake her hand.

'St… Stan? My Stan?' she said. 'Oh my gawd, just look at you! What 'ave you got on?'

'Eh? It's my suit, my demob suit, nice ain't…'

'Bit tight under the arms, didn't they 'ave one your…' She turned and called into the house "Ere, Bill, guess who's back! It's my Stan, he's come home and don't he look a picture! Come on son, you better come in.'

'Okay! Ma…'

Stan paused on the doorstep and grabbed her gently by the elbow. He looked at her inquisitively.

'…where's Dad? Who's Bill?'

She looked back and shook her head.

'Got some explaining to do, ain't I? Come on, it's alright.'

They walked to the front room and Gladys took up a defensive position behind Bill who was seated at the dining table. She rested her hands on his shoulders and spoke solemnly.

'Stan, this is Bill. Bill, my Stan.'

'Afternoon!' said Stan.

'Alright, son?' replied Bill. 'Back from playing at soldiers, then, eh? Mug's game that.'

'No. I've been fighting for my country. When did you get out?'

'Out? Out! 'Ere Gladys, you 'ear that? He's asking when I got out! Ain't never been in, son. Like I says, mug's game.'

'How come?'

'How come? What is this? Bleedin' inquisition? You been hanging round with the Reich or what?'

'No, no. I just meant…'

'Flat feet, ain't I. Ha! Won't take ya if ya got flat feet.'

'What about the other corps? Home Office, or, or…'

'Now you be careful son, who do you think you…'

'Stan,' said Gladys, 'Bill's been looking after me, he's a good sort, don't go off on one, not when you just got back like.'

Stan looked at Bill. He was forty-ish and wore a pencil moustache. His hair was slicked back and his ears stuck out. He sat with his shirt sleeves rolled to just above the elbow and the remnants of a sausage supper sat on his plate. He picked his teeth and eyed Stan with disdain. Animosity filled the air as they squared up to each other.

'So, anything to eat, Ma?' asked Stan. 'I'm starving! Don't get much in the mess, know what I mean!'

'Course, son. You sit down and I'll bring ya something. Got some beans left I think.'

'Beans? What, no sausages?'

'Oh, Bill's had 'em. Sorry luv.'

'Bill's had 'em, eh? What else has Bill 'ad?'

'Now just you watch your mouth, son, war or no war, if your father was around…'

'Yeah? Where is Dad, Ma? Where is he?'

'He's… he's gone away.'

'What do you mean, gone away?'

'He's passed on.'

'What?! When?'

'Coupla years ago, nearly, during a raid it was. He was over the river. Went down Bethnal Green tube, to shelter like. Got trampled to death. Terrible it was.'

'I don't believe it! He was just, he was…'

'I know son, but life goes on. Sit yourself down, back in a tick.'

Stan looked at his Mum and slowly the anger welled inside him. His eyes darted between Gladys and Bill.

'Nearly two years eh? And you didn't think to write?'

'Well, you know what it's like, with the doodlebugs and things, I never got the…'

'Two years. You finished mourning, Ma? How long's Bill been 'ere?'

Bill rose to his feet and slammed his fist on the table.

'Now you listen 'ere!' he yelled. 'You're not too old for a cuff round the ear, you know. Don't think I wouldn't…'

'But old enough to fight for my country, for me Ma, for freedom. And old enough to lay you out if come near me.'

'I'm warning you boy!'

'Fuck off!' yelled Stan, 'Just fuck off! I'm going down the boozer, and you better be gone when I get back!'

'Oi! I call the shots round 'ere, I…'

'You!' Stan lowered his voice to a barely audible whisper, 'You have no place in this 'ouse. I'm warning you. I've killed men. I've killed other human beings, one more ain't gonna make no difference, not to me. Do you understand?'

Bill sat down, silently. His face was ashen with fear, all his bravado was drawn to the seat of his pants. He kept his eyes on Stan but said no more. Inwardly, he contemplated moving on. Gladys was shocked, her son had returned a man, in more ways than one. She made a feeble attempt to reconcile their differences.

'Stan, don't…' she said.

Her words hung in the air as the door slammed behind him. Homecomings weren't what they were cracked up to be.

He pulled his hat down low over his brow and strode purposefully along the street. His addled mind struggled to get to grips with the loss of his father, his mother dressed to the nines on a weekday afternoon and a stranger muscling in on his home. He took solace in the fact that the Thomas à Becket was still standing and barged through the door with the force of Enola Gay's fly-by over Hiroshima.

The pub fell silent, all eyes fell upon him, the eyes of strangers. There were no young men to be seen, just old folk supping pints of bitter that lasted for hours. Rationing was biting hard and simple pleasures were few and far between. He ambled to the bar and ordered a beer, desperate for solitude and the opportunity to wrangle with the mayhem in his mind. Gradually, the sound of conversation returned to normal and he was forgotten.

He looked about him. Like his home, the pub hadn't changed. It smelled of stale dogs and ashtrays, strands of shag littered the floor and the piano stood idle in the corner. The only thing missing was the laughter that used to fill its heaving bars.

He drank with a thirst that would ensure inebriation was swift; and eight week's pay would last a fortnight. He ordered a second pint just as a wily, old man approached him with a quizzical look on his face. Stan looked skyward and spoke begrudgingly.

'Go on then, old timer, what ya havin'?'

'Eh?' said the old man. 'I don't want nothin', you're… you're… go on then. Large Scotch.'

'That's an expensive nothin', you'll have me broke before…'

'You're Gladys' boy, ain't ya? Stanley, right?'

'Yeah, yeah. Sorry granddad, do I know…'

'Tom, next but one. We used to go to…'

'Go to church together! Every Sunday!'

'S'right.'

Stan's face glowed with relief. At last he'd found one of the old crowd, a friendly face.

'Bugger me! Sorry Tom, I didn't recognise ya! What the bloody hell ya doin' now?'

'Not much son, lost the 'ouse, lost the lot. One minute it was quiet, next thing all I hear is this almighty wheeeeeeeee. On the carsey at the time, legged it with me trousers round me ankles, must've looked a picture!'

'Oh, Tom, I'm sorry mate, don't mean to laugh, but ya gotta admit…'

'Yeah, I know, s'alright. You just got back, son? Bad, was it?'

'Bad? Yeah, it was bad. Bloody awful in fact.'

'Worse than the first I bet, and I know what I'm talkin' about.'

'I know ya do. Here, cheers. Good to see ya, Tom.'

They clinked glasses, chatted about North Africa and the Blitz and what they'd give for a bacon sandwich. Tom stared into his second Scotch as he spoke.

'Been 'ome yet, Stan?'

'Yeah, just been. Some 'omecomin' that was, make no mistake.'

'Shame. Could've warned ya.'

'Warned me? 'bout what? Me Ma?'

'That. Lot of things really.'

'Go on Tom, I'm listening.'

'Know about your old man?'

'Yeah, yeah. I…'

'Don't worry son, bad luck, that's all. Good man he was. We'll miss him. Well, most of us.'

'Ha! You're talkin' 'bout Ma, right?'

'It's not my place, I shouldn't…'

'It's okay, Tom, really, it's okay. Go on.'

'Well, that Bill geezer, he ain't the first. After your old man copped it, she was distraught, really bad like, couldn't cope. You off fightin', her husband dead. She needed support.'

'Who wouldn't?'

'Right. But these geezers that came and went, they was just takin' advantage. Bought her things, chocolate, stockings, you know the like. It's not her fault, she just got a taste for it, that's all. Liked livin' a life of luxury.'

'I understand, Tom. Thanks.'

'No. No son, ya don't understand. The geezer that's there now, he's the sixth this year. I'm sorry son, she's… she's takin' men in, know what I mean?'

'Nah! You're kidding! You mean she's…'

'She's offering her services.'

'For what? A quick wotsit for… for a coupla chops? Is that what you're sayin'?'

'Fraid so. I'm sorry.'

'So who knows? Everyone? I suppose everyone's looking at me cos me mum's a bleedin' whore!'

'No, no, it ain't that bad, but I thought you should hear it from me like, not gossip. You know what they're like round 'ere.'

'Yeah. Thanks, Tom. Jesus, really, thanks.'

'Talk to her, son. I've tried, God knows I've tried, but she don't listen to me. She needs ya, Stan. She needs something solid back in her life. You talk to her, you set her straight. Go on.'

'Right you are. I'll see ya.'

Stan downed his pint, promised to look in on Tom at the shelter and strolled back home. The war had changed him. He had so much pent-up anger he felt he could explode at any moment. He had expected, or rather, wanted, to return to some tea and sympathy, to some friendly faces, some breathing space and the opportunity to off-load everything that troubled him with someone who understood. Instead he had to cope with feeling like an unwanted guest at a party, a mother on the game and a father he would never see again.

He contemplated his mother's career move and instead of anger, he felt nothing but sorrow. He almost understood the reasons why, almost convinced himself such reasons were legitimate and ignored the fact that she was the only woman doing it in this neck of the woods. He assured himself that her actions were nothing more than a confused and temporary aberration and vowed to restore what was left of his family to its former values.

Warily, he approached the front door. Still keyless, he knocked lightly, stupidly fearful he may wake someone. Gladys opened the door and looked genuinely pleased to see him.

'Oh, Stan! I'm sorry, luv. Come on, I got something special for ya dinner.'

'I'm sorry too, Ma. Er, where's… is Bill…?'

'He's gone. Just you and me now, son.'

'As it should be, Ma. As it should be.'

* * *

Stan planted himself at the dining table where Gladys presented him with a bottle of stout before disappearing to the kitchen. He sipped slowly and pored over the 'situations vacant' in the newspaper. They were few and far between. Before long, she returned with his dinner: two pork chops and a mountain of peas swimming in Oxo gravy.

'Ma! Bloody fantastic! I ain't seen… where'd it come from?'

'Leaving present, from you know who.'

'In that case, best not waste it, eh?'

'Eat up son. Must be a long time since you've had a decent meal.'

'Too right. Can't beat a bit of home-cooking.'

'I'll look after ya, don't you worry. Need building up, you do. Look at ya, scrawny you are.'

'I'm fine. Listen, we don't have to do this every night, okay?' he said, pointing at his plate. 'Everyone else has to make do, so, so can we.'

'Us? Make do? Do you know what it's like eating rubbish every day? You got any idea how long those coupons last?'

'Yes, Ma! Yes, I know what it's like to eat crap every day, worse crap than you've had to eat. I know rationing is tough, but we can get by. We can do without… you don't have to…'

'Have to what?'

Stan put down his cutlery and looked his mum square in the eye.

'I've been talking to Tom.'

'Tom? What's he got do with the price of eggs?'

'Everything. He told me everything.'

A look of recognition and embarrassment flashed across her face.

'Interfering old fool! I'll bleedin' well…'

'No, Ma, you won't. It's okay, we're okay. I'm back, you don't have to…'

'I'm sorry! You must think I'm a right tart, they're all talkin' about me.'

'No, Ma, they ain't, and you ain't.'

'I didn't know what to do, I had to get on, I had to…'

'And now ya don't. It's okay, I understand. Let's put it behind us and move on, alright?'

'You're good sort, Stan. You've turned out alright, you have.'

'Thanks to you. Now, subject closed. I'm gonna eat Bill's legacy and set about looking for a job, alright?'

'Old man Llewellyn.'

'Eh?'

'You know, off Trafalgar Avenue, he needs help.'

'Really? I thought he'd snuffed it years ago.'

'Don't be daft. Go see him, he's busy, lotta work for chippies right now.'

'Chippies? I ain't a bloody carpenter ma, how am…'

'You can learn, can't ya?'

'Yeah, yeah, s'pose I can.'

* * *

Stan went to bed a happy man. Not only had he reconciled what was left of his family, he was confident about the job too. After all, he'd known Llewellyn as a boy, he'd snap him up, surely, a man of his experience.

Chapter Two

The desert shimmered in a fuzzy, heat haze. Streams of sweat trickled gently down his cheeks. Flies swarmed over limbless bodies and the stench of fear filled his nostrils. The incessant sound of artillery fire rattled between his ears and echoed in his head. He turned to the lad on his right. They stared at each other, wide-eyed like abandoned Golliwogs. They were terrified. He looked away, pulled his helmet down over his eyebrows, bowed his head and prayed.

* * *

He woke with a start. It was a little after six. The pillow was drenched. He could taste salt on his lips. He cracked his knuckles and took a deep breath. He had no appetite for breakfast, instead he bathed, dressed and waited at the yard for over an hour until the Welshman showed up.

Llewellyn had changed slightly about the face. He was still rotund but the shiny, smiley head that once graced his shoulders was replaced with that of a war-weary soul who'd spent too many sleepless nights telling folk to 'turn that bloody light out!' He recognised Stan in a thrice, his Rhondda baritone boomed with delight.

'Stanley Wilkins! Bloody hell, you've grown, boy! Looking at a man, so I am.'

'Alright, Mr Llewellyn! How's it…'

'Mister? There's formal, isn't it? You've got manners though, boy, tell you that for nothing. You're old enough to call me, Gareth, I think.'

'Thanks. I…'

'Don't tell me. You want a job, right?'

'Well…'

'You're hired. Blinkin' run off my feet like you wouldn't believe. Go home and change, no room for a suit here, my lad.'

'Thanks Mr… Gareth! I… I… I'll be back before…'

'Before the kettle's boiled, I know.'

* * *

Stan returned to the yard to find Llewellyn sitting on a crate, Woodbine in one hand and a mug of tea in the other.

'That was quick,' he said. 'Keen, aren't you?'

'Yessir! Not afraid of hard work me, I can do anything.'

'Good. Well, look around you. This is what we call the yard, and that there see, is what we call a broom. Know how it works, do you?'

'Leave it to me! By the way, where is everyone, your men, like?'

'On site mainly. Or in the workshop, prepping, round the back. Preparation is everything. We cut the timber, fashion the mouldings, make the glue, then out it goes, on the lorry. You'll see them around, boy. Get to know them in time, you will.'

'Gotcha. S'pose I'll be here then?'

'Oh yes! You'll be here alright, need six of you, so I do. Dare say you'll learn a thing or two while you're at it. Now, when you've put that broom through its paces, come find me. And listen, drink that tea before it gets cold.'

The yard was spotless. If nothing else, Stan was a man who took pride in his work, whatever the task. He found Llewellyn in the boiler room, huddled over a steaming vat which smelled of all things rancid.

'Phwoar! What a stink!' said Stan. 'Hope that's not your dinner!'

'There's funny. Member of the concert party, were we? This is glue, boy, strong enough to hold your house up, it is, and you'll be making it every day.'

'Thanks. What the bleedin' hell's in there?'

'Oh, let's see, bones, bit of skin, few teeth, tendons…'

'Okay, okay, seriously. I want to learn!'

'Never been more serious in my life, lad. Now, take note…'

He did. Two weeks passed and Stan studiously maintained a notebook which he crammed with the tricks of the trade. He soon became proficient in the manufacture of animal glue. He learned the difference between a coping saw, a tenon saw and a panel saw. He could handle a block plane, a bullnose plane and a rebate plane. He knew when and where to use an oval brad, a lost head or a clout, and he could spot a dovetail a mile off.

Stan was doing the work of two men, even three, without complaint and with enthusiasm. Llewellyn was clearly impressed. He made his feelings known at the end of his two week probation period and presented Stan with his first wage packet. Two week's pay, one week's bonus and the offer of permanent work.

Stan was overjoyed. What was left of his demob pay didn't add up to much and he wanted desperately to give his mum whatever she needed. The ration coupons didn't cover everything and bread alone was running at 4d a loaf.

By way of celebration, he decided to award himself a couple of jars in the Thomas à Becket. He stopped at the bakers on the way and squandered one shilling and sixpence on an almond cake and 4d on two chocolate bars, confident it would bring a smile to his Ma's face.

The pub was dead, which was unusual for a Friday night, but Stan was quietly pleased. He didn't relish idle banter and was sick to death of hearing 'Roll out the Barrel'. He spied old Tom nursing a pint in the corner, bought him a Scotch, and went over. They chatted eagerly about Stan's new career and how well his mum was coping now that he was back. On that subject Tom remained nonchalant and advised Stan not to get his hopes up. Perplexed, and somewhat the worse for the beer, Stan left Tom a tanner for a drink and weaved his way back home.

He fumbled for his keys, giggling as he did so, and eventually fell into the house. Gladys was sat at the dining table, clad only in a dressing gown and smoking a cigarette.

'Ooh Stan! Where 'ave you been?' she said. 'Look at the state of ya!'

'Just a bit merry, Ma, that's all! Look, present for ya, ta-daa! Cake!'

'Cake? Where'd…'

'Chocolate!'

'Choc…what 'ave you…'

'Paypacket! Three weeks' pay! Old Llewellyn, he's my boss, he says... he says I am the best thing that's ever...'

'Oh Stan, you are a sight! Sit yourself down, son, I'll get your dinner, probably turned by now.'

Gladys returned with a plate of Woolton Pie.

'Lovely Ma!' he spurted out between mouthfuls. 'So, what ya doin' up so late anyway? You should be in bed.'

'Waiting for you! Wanted to tell ya, going away ain't I, just for the weekend like. Got an early start.'

'Bloody great! Good for you! Where ya goin'?'

'Margate.'

'Lovely! You, Ma, you deserve it. I'll be up early, don't you worry. I'll take ya to the station, Charing Cross ain't it?'

'S'alright son, I'll get...'

'Gladys!'

The voice came from the hallway. Eloquent and clipped. A small man, fifty-ish in years, sauntered into the room. He was dressed in pin-striped trousers and wore his braces over a singlet.

'Gladys, there you are, come on, aren't you...?'

Stan spat a mouthful of food onto plate as his anger threatened to spill. Gladys spoke while she had the chance.

'Stan, this is Archie, he's taking me to Margate. He's got a motor car. It's alright Stan, we're just... companions. Companions, that's all.'

'And I thought...' said Stan, '...and I thought.'

His words drifted into space. He contemplated throwing Archie out on the street but something told him he wasn't entirely to blame. He thought of what Tom had said in the pub and wanted to call his mother a slag. Instead, he wiped his mouth with the back of his hand, shot daggers at the banker in the vest and wished them a pleasant trip. The solace of his bed was all he craved, that, and to wake up sober, a part of a normal family.

* * *

The force of the blast knocked him clean off his feet, showering him in sand and dust. Instinctively, he covered his head with his hands and lay face down, completely still. His heart pounded like a piston engine at full pelt. The troop carrier had taken a direct hit. Screams of desperation filled the air. 'Get them out!' bellowed the staff sergeant. He jumped up and ran towards the blazing wreckage. A soldier, the same age as him, was hanging off the bonnet with a gaping hole in his belly. Stan froze. What he saw was meant to be inside the body, not poking out. 'Shove it back in and get 'im to the bloody tent!' yelled the sergeant. Stan swore under his breath. The intestine was like a flaccid water balloon, wobbling and pulsing. It was warm and wet and it stank. Stan grew flustered as he tried to grip it, tried to stop it slithering in his hands. He pushed it back in to a crimson mire and wiped his brow with the blood of a dead man.

* * *

He woke with a jolt and sat bolt upright. His bowels felt loose. The room was black as pitch and his head pounded like a Panzer. He took a deep breath and sat on his hands to stop them trembling. It was eleven o'clock. The house was quiet. His mother had left. He pulled the curtains and allowed his eyes to adjust to the glare of the sun. A wave of nausea washed over his icy face. A fry-up at the café or a few bits from the shop would see him right. He dressed. His patience wore thin as he searched for his paypacket. He had left it on the kitchen table. He swore blind he'd left it on the kitchen table. His anger bubbled like a festering cauldron of frustration as he scoured the cupboards and the drawers, his pockets, his coat and even his mother's bedroom. It was nowhere to be seen. It had gone. Then it hit him. Like a freight train. Three week's pay was somewhere in Margate.

His bloodshot eyes groaned with the weight of the sun as he queued for bread. The women ahead of him turned and giggled and whispered amongst themselves. He was too ashamed to stay. Too angry for dough. A hair of the dog would do him more good than a slice of toast. He headed for the pub.

'You're early, young Stanley,' said the landlord. 'Usual?'

'Ta,' replied Stan.

He contemplated his pint. It smelled of mildew and tasted of hate. He almost gagged as he forced the first gulp down.

Two builders were sat at the bar. They were grubby and tired and already drunk. They nudged each other and giggled like schoolboys. The one nearest Stan looked over and called down the bar.

'Alright, Wilky!' he said, raising his glass.

Stan glanced up. He'd never seen them before.

'Fine,' he said.

'Good, that's good. Oi Wilky, where's yer mum? She out working?'

They both spluttered into their beer. Stan said nothing. The other one chipped in, his tone aggressive.

'Oi, ain't you got no manners? He just asked you a question, he said where's yer mum?'

Stan lifted his head and glared at the feral inebriates. He lowered his gaze and scratched at the varnish on the beer-stained bar with his fingernail. He frowned and spoke quietly. Confidently.

'I don't want a fight,' he said, 'but if I have to, I will kill you.'

'You what? I'm gonna tear your bloody block off, you…'

The builder tried to stand and clutched his mate for support. Stan stood tall, downed his pint and smashed the glass on the bar.

'Who's first?' he whispered, his vacuous eyes as dark as the gateway to hell.

'That's enough!' yelled the barmaid.

She stepped from behind the bar and swaggered towards the builders, hands on hips. At little more than five feet tall, she was a scrawny lass with gamine features and close-cropped hair, but as a barmaid she knew how to stand her ground.

'This is a pub!' she bellowed. 'Not a hostel for sad, single drunks, now get the feck out! You're barred!'

They said nothing, sneered at Stan and knocked over a stool as a gesture of defiance as they staggered out. Eileen cocked her head at Stan, smiled and took the broken glass from his hand.

'Thanks,' said Stan, 'but you didn't have to. I'll pay for the glass.'

'Don't be daft, we don't want the likes of them in here anyway, you did me a favour.'

'I would've killed 'em. Trust me.'

'Course ya would. So, you must be Stanley Wilkins, I assume?'

'S'right. You assume correctly. Stan. And you are…'

'Eileen,' she said, flashing a wide grin. 'Eileen Doyle, who finishes work in an hour. Stick around and you can buy me a drink if ya like.'

Stan chuckled quietly and shook his head.

'I'd like that. Yes, okay, I'd like that very much.'

* * *

Eileen was three years Stan's senior but she didn't look it. She was single and pretty, naturally so, but no-one took a shine to her because she refused to dress in pretty frocks and high heels. Hers was the look of a land girl. Made no difference to Stan, the clothes didn't bother him, she did. He was spellbound. She joined him at the table and they sat and chatted for hours. She was born in Mile End. Her parents had travelled from County Laois – 'that's bogland to you!' – in the early Twenties to ensure their only child had the chance of a brighter future. It didn't go according to plan. Two years later they both contracted tuberculosis and passed away within a month of each other. Eileen was raised by Barnardo's in Stepney. As soon as she was old enough, she left to make her own way in the world, well, London anyway. With nothing more than a basic education and a good set of morals, she'd worked her way round most of the pubs in the East End before arriving at the Thomas à Becket six months earlier. She was a strong, independent, self-assured lass who could fend for herself. That impressed Stan. He thought his own life sounded dull by comparison. Average house on an average street, single parent and no mates. He knew he couldn't sweep her off her feet. Who'd have him when there were much more interesting lads around?

* * *

It was getting late. Stan offered to walk Eileen home. The very least he could do was make the most of her company while he had the chance. They shared a bag of chips all the way to her front door. He looked up at the house, expecting the curtains to twitch, the landlady to scowl. It didn't happen.

'Well, here you are then,' said Stan. 'Home. Safe and sound. In one piece. Ta, for a nice night and all, I enjoyed it.'

'That sounds like a "I don't want to see you again speech" if ever I heard one.'

'No!' said Stan. 'I thought…'

She rose on tiptoe and gave him a peck on the cheek.

'In that case, you can take out me out again,' she said.

* * *

Monday morning. Stan arrived early at the yard with a favour to ask of Llewellyn. He needed an advance, a sub. He was too embarrassed to say where the best part of three weeks' wages had gone and consequently enjoyed a gentle lecture from old man Llewellyn on how to manage money.

'Look, I know you've been through a lot lad, and goodness knows, I don't envy you, not for one minute. It's going to take a long time for you to come to terms with what you've seen, but the answer's not at the bottom of a bottle, understand? Just take it easy, like. No-one's begrudging you a drink son, you've bloody well earned it, but take it easy.'

He liked Llewellyn and his fatherly advice. All week long he worked like a dog, tirelessly, even through his lunch break. It was his way of thanking Llewellyn and it didn't go unnoticed.

'Stanley!' bellowed old man Llewellyn, 'now, here's the thing, see. I like the fact you're here early, so, you carry on and you can knock off at four, how's that? And for your troubles – cos you're not a bloody milkman, right? – there's an extra few bob in it. How does that sound?'

'Thanks Gareth, Mr Llewellyn, ta! I like coming in early, I mean, it's quiet ain't it? Peaceful.'

'Good lad! Here, you'll be needing these, I expect you to open up every morning and don't bloody lose them whatever you do!'

He handed Stan a set of keys and with them a sense of responsibility.

* * *

Saturday. It may have been the weekend but there was no lie-in for Stan. He was up with the larks and landed himself pole position at the head of the queue outside the butchers. It didn't matter how much money he had in his pocket, rationing meant he could only get a shilling's worth of meat. He grabbed three pounds of lamb and headed home. He polished off a breakfast of bacon, eggs, black pudding and toast washed down with a cup of splosh. He sat with his feet up and enjoyed the solitude. He liked it on his own, with no-one to annoy him he felt settled and calm and dozed off till the mantle clock woke him with a start. It was five o'clock. He pulled on a clean shirt, brushed his hair and raced up to the pub.

Sitting with his back to the bar, he gazed out on to the street and thought of nothing. Eileen walked up behind him, gently placed her hands over his eyes and whispered:

'Stanley Wilkins I presume?'

He smiled.

'Shall we?'

They strolled up to the Regal which had emerged from the Blitz unscathed. They sat at the back, engulfed by cigarette smoke and watched 'Dead of Night'. Eileen slipped her arm round Stan's and held him tight. He liked that. He liked the thought of protecting her from things that went bump in the night.

Afterwards, he walked her home.

'You working tomorrow?' he asked.

'Nope, Sunday is my day of rest… why do you ask?'

Stan took a deep breath.

'Well, if you ain't got any plans, like, thought maybe we could, we could have some dinner. Sunday dinner? If you fancy it?'

'Stanley Wilkins, I'd love to!'

'Smashing! I got some lamb.'

'Grand!'

'Er, don't suppose you know how to cook, do you? Lamb I mean.'

'Bloody cheek! Alright, call for me.'

They faced each other, bathed in yellow street light, and kissed. Stan waited till she closed the door and ran all the way home. He flopped into bed, crossed his hands behind his head and gazed up at the ceiling. He pictured Eileen's face and drifted off to sleep.

* * *

Stan stared in disbelief at what was left of it and swallowed hard to keep the bile down. A fragment of bony shin and a mass of shredded, pink tissue hung from below the knee. Flies hovered, eager to feast on the raw meat.

'Hold it lad, go on, hold it tight, we 'aven't got all day.'

He looked at the leg.

'Can't sir,' he whispered, his mouth as dry as the surrounding desert.

'Hold it before we bloody well lose him! Now!'

Stan placed both hands on the thigh and gripped it tight. It was warm and sticky like the syrup on a sponge pudding. He closed his eyes as he heard the saw hack through the bone. The rasp of the blade made him flinch with every stroke. Then it stopped. He opened his eyes and stood back. The shin was gone. The knee was gone. The blood collected in a pool under the weeping stump. First he smelled the morphine, then the acrid stench of burning flesh and the sizzle of pan-fried bacon as they cauterised the wound. He couldn't take anymore. He ran outside and puked.

* * *

His feet were cold. His pyjamas, damp. He got up and lit a cigarette, fearful if he returned to bed, sleep would envelope him in another merciless memory.

* * *

It was just after one when he called for Eileen. He was dressed in his best, and only, suit. She was wearing a frock, a white frock covered in pink roses. It was the first time he, or anyone else, had seen her ankles.

'You, you look a picture!' he said.

They walked, arm in arm, over to Stan's house. He gave her the grand tour, ending in the kitchen where he ceremoniously dumped three pounds of lamb on the table. Eileen donned an apron, unwrapped the paper and picked at the contents.

'Scrag,' she said.

'Eh?'

'Scrag end. Enough for a week. Think we'll have a stew, come on you, spuds need peeling.'

The rich, warm smell that came from the pot permeated every room in the house. Its comforting aroma made it feel like a home. They nestled together on the couch, sipping ale, while it slowly simmered away. Eileen was curious about Stan. She'd met a fair few lads who had been at the Front. They were damaged goods, infected by a war-borne virus that sapped their self-esteem. They drank and swore and cried at night, too proud to ask for help. By contrast, Stan seemed level-headed, conscientious, normal. It didn't seem right. She wondered about his scars and how deeply he had buried them. She wondered what was ticking in his head. He was staring into space. He looked like a UXB.

'I'm alright, love,' he said, 'don't worry about me, just did me job, like the rest of 'em. S'pose I can cope with it better, that's all. Funny thing is, I wasn't even meant to be with the Meds. I was 10th Armoured.'

'So what happened?' she asked.

'What happened is I 'appened to be in the wrong bleedin' place at the wrong bleedin' time! Carrier took a hit, see, so I dragged a couple of lads off to the medics…'

'You rescued them, I mean saved them?'

'Yeah, s'pose so. Anyway, I got collared didn't I, they needed a hand so I helped 'em out. Got a bit carried away. 10th never came looking for me, so I stayed with them.'

'So you're a doctor, then?'

'No love, not me. I just did what they told me to. After a while you pick it up, don't ya? Can't say it was the best job I ever had but you just get on with it, become immune to it after a while. Tell ya what though, if old man Llewellyn gives me the elbow, I could always be a butcher!'

It had grown dark outside. 'Variety Bandbox' blew trumpets from the wireless and the standard lamp flicked shadows gently across the room. Stan fetched a deck of cards and they played Gin Rummy while he told her about his mother. 'Best to clear the air, like. No surprises. Anyway, looks like she ain't coming back.' Eileen felt for him. She'd landed herself a goodun in Stanley Wilkins. Thoughtful, compassionate and a war hero to boot. She kicked off her shoes and snuggled up close.

'Take me dancing next week, if you like,' she said.

Stan nodded off. She gave him half an hour and nudged him back to consciousness.

'It's late,' she said, 'and you look done in. Better get yourself a good night's sleep, Stanley Wilkins. Anyway, I should get going, don't want the neighbours talking, do we?'

'Neighbours? Ain't got any!' he said.

They laughed, caught each other's eyes and stopped abruptly. They kissed.

'Now I really should go,' she said, 'before I get myself in trouble!'

'Shame. I always liked getting into trouble. C'mon, I'll walk you.'

He waited till Eileen was safely inside and ambled back home with just the moon for company. He felt light-headed, intoxicated, almost delirious. The street was deserted. He paused at his front door, key in lock, and momentarily pictured Eileen on the couch inside, waiting for him with a smile.

* * *

Tirelessly, he dragged body after body to the medics' tent, each one heavier than the last. Some groaned, some cried, some prayed, the others were silent, nothing more than a putrid, tangled mess of organs decaying in the scorching heat. He laid them out in neat rows, face down like sardines, to prevent them from rotting in the sun. He was impervious to the sight of vomit, immune to the reek of excrement, hardened to the desperate pleas for help. It was the noise he hated. The incessant boom of the guns. The roar of the shells as they exploded. Bang! Bang! Bang! Shell after shell after shell. Bang! Bang! Bang!

He opened his eyes, fists clenched tight. His brow dripped with sweat. Still, the thunder of shells continued. He clenched his teeth, willing the noise to stop. Suddenly, the door flew open. Startled, he whipped round to face her. She stood, stock still, silhouetted by the light in the hall.

'You deaf or something?' yelled his mother. 'I've been bangin' that door for bleedin' ages!'

He didn't hear her. He grabbed the quilt with both hands and pulled it to his face. Swirling clouds of panic swept around his mind. The sun shone bright behind her. Another shell exploded in his ears. She stepped forward and slowly raised her hand. A bayonet finger reached for the light switch. A flare extinguished the night. Screaming, he leapt from the bed and charged at her, head low. He knocked her from her feet and her head hit the wall with a single, dull thud. Suddenly, the shelling stopped. The guns fell silent. He watched as she slumped slowly to the floor, a crimson stream marked her descent. The helmet had fallen to one side, the khaki fatigues were shredded with shrapnel. Blood trickled lethargically from her nose. He reached down, grabbed her by the collar and dragged her to the bathroom.

'Another one, Sarge!' he said, and went back to bed.

Chapter Three

Five o'clock. Alarm bells pealed and Stan struggled to get out of bed, his body heavy with fatigue. He switched on the light and sat at the dresser. The bags under his eyes were like the contours on a map of the Lake District. He stuck out his tongue, yawned and placed a hand on his chest. His heart was racing.

Gladys Wilkins remained motionless. Her head rested on the back of tub, her eyes, white. Congealed blood formed a crusty track of lava down her chin. Stan knelt beside her and studied her face. His lip curled at the mole on her cheek which sprouted a single, grey hair. He closed her eyes and wept. Silent tears fell, drop by drop, to the floor.

'I'm sorry, Ma. It was an accident. I should never 'ave come back, then none of this would've 'appened and you'd still be here.'

He paused. His eyes narrowed. He could taste venom on his tongue.

'You'd still be here, shagging every bloke sad enough to 'ave you. Selling yourself for a pair of nylons or 'alf a pound of best end. What would Dad've said, eh? Tell me that. Poor bastard. What happened to you, Ma? What turned you into a thieving whore? Why'd ya come back? You run out of money?'

He walked to the door and looked back at her.

'Don't go anywhere,' he said. 'I'll sort you out later.'

* * *

Stan's mind was in turmoil. He couldn't call the police, even if it was an accident, they'd have him banged up in no time. He couldn't tell Eileen and he couldn't tell Llewellyn. Or could he? He was an understanding chap. He'd known him all his life. No. He could tell no-one. It was up to him to rid the tub of betrayal.

It was four o'clock and Llewellyn had had enough. His protégé's mind was not on the job, he sent him home early. 'Get some rest lad, you're done in, you are.'

Stan shuffled home, distraught at his dilemma, pondering a possible solution. He stopped opposite the house and then it struck him. It was obvious. No-one had actually seen his mother return. Moreover, she'd returned alone. Late. So far as anyone was concerned, she was still in Margate. He knew what he had to do. And he had three bottles of stout in the cupboard to help him do it.

The smell of coal filled the chilly, evening air. Chimneys puffed plumes of smoggy smoke into the dusk. It was perfect. He ran inside, pulled the curtains and drank a beer as the fire hissed and crackled into life. Upstairs, Gladys was in the first throes of rigor mortis. Her skin was the colour of fag ash. She was clammy and cold to the touch. He relieved her of her earrings, her necklace and an amethyst brooch pinned to her blouse, placed them in a tobacco tin and hid it in his sock drawer. Her clothes weren't so easy to remove. He tore the garments from her rigid limbs till she was completely naked, took them downstairs and piled them onto the fire. He sipped his second beer as they went up in smoke then took the bread knife and a bottle of Teachers up to the bathroom. He sat on the bath, took a couple of slugs of whisky and scowled at Gladys.

'Ready when you are, Sarge,' he said.

'Good lad,' came the silent reply.

The skin on her neck was saggy and wrinkled, like a farmyard turkey. The blade struggled to get a purchase. He yanked her head back and sliced more vigorously, long, confident strokes, till he hit the vertebrae. He dropped the knife, grabbed her head with both hands and gave it a short, sharp twist. It cracked like a festive walnut. There was little blood. He ripped it off and wrapped it in a copy of the Daily Mirror. It resembled a papier maché football, ready for painting.

Crudely, but deftly, he set about dismembering her from the feet up. He lifted her leg and sliced around her ankle, deep enough to sever the tendons. It was as if he'd uncorked a keg of beer, the blood flowed effortlessly toward the plughole. 'Fancy another? Don't mind if I do.' He lifted the other leg, repeated the process and waited for the remnants of life to drain away. A slug of whisky. Another twist, and each foot was liberated from its leg. He wrapped them in news of Goering's suicide and placed them next to the football.

The foot bone connected to the leg bone,
The leg bone connected to the knee bone,

The knee bone connected to the thigh bone.
Not any more, it ain't.

Before long he was done. He carried her down to the cellar and laid her out on the trestle table, fetched the cleaver from the kitchen and set about chopping each limb into smaller parts, separating the toes from the feet, the fingers from the hands, the ribs from the sternum.

Dem bones, dem bones, dem dry bones,
Now hear the word of the Lord.

He wrapped each part in newspaper and placed them in his mother's wicker shopper. Finally, he scooped up her innards.

Chopped liver, sir?
No ta, think I'll 'ave a cold heart.

He pushed the football on top and was surprised at how little space a body occupied when it was in pieces. He cleaned the cellar, removed all evidence of his impromptu surgery and went upstairs to wash his tools. He scrubbed the bathroom from top to bottom until it was immaculate then drank his last of bottle of beer while he pokered up the fire. She was gone. He felt no guilt. No remorse. In fact, he could hardly remember doing it.

There was one more chore to take care of before he went to bed. His room. It was a tip. Despite his lassitude he soldiered on, for Eileen's sake. He stuffed his clothes in the laundry basket, ran a duster over the dresser and went downstairs for the umpteenth time to fetch the Hoover. The carpet came up a treat, till he ran it under the bed and something jammed inside it. He cursed, turned it on its side and retrieved the obstacle. It was an envelope. A small, brown envelope. A wage packet. Complete with nearly three weeks' pay.

* * *

It was early. Not even the milkman was up yet. The puddles rippled as his boots click-clacked along Trafalgar Avenue. He set the basket on the ground and opened the gates. He went straight to the boiler room, fired up the vat and unwrapped what remained of Mrs Wilkins. Gently, he stirred her into the gunk and pushed the football to the bottom. By the end of the day there'd be nothing identifiable left. At the end of the week, when he raked it out, the bones would be ground up and sold on as fertiliser. He sat back with a cup of tea. 'Think I'll do a spot of decorating,' he said to himself.

* * *

The following night Eileen was waiting for him. He liked to do things properly, what he called 'the old-fashioned way'. That meant calling for his girl and seeing her home. Eileen liked that. She liked the maturity of his manners and his chivalrous ways. It made her feel safe, special, wanted. She liked having a reason to dress up. He was punctual, as usual. Six o'clock, on the button. They walked, arm in arm, to The Frog and Nightgown. Stan led her through the throngs of wheelers and dealers to the snug at the back of the bar. They whiled away a couple of hours, six pints of Best and two port and lemon before heading home. They stopped for haddock and chips on the way, his treat, and scoffed it on the couch, straight from the paper. Eileen curled up beside him as the wireless crackled to life. Casually, he stretched his arm around her and stroked her breast.

'Stanley Wilkins!' she said. 'What kind of a girl do you think I am!'

He dropped his hand, she laughed and put it back, this time under her blouse. They kissed and he began to undress her.

'Not now, Stan, next time. Properly, when you haven't had a skinful!'

He smiled.

* * *

Stan took pride in his work, all week long he toiled like a trouper, but he was becoming bored. He wanted Llewellyn to move him up the ladder, he wanted to be a craftsman. He wanted a skill, a talent, something he could use to invest in a future. He idled and pictured a shop, nothing grand, but it had a sign above the window: 'S. Wilkins and Son, Carpentry and Joinery'. He'd never even thought about kids, but it sounded good. Friday morning reminded him of who he really was: the general hand who opened up the yard.

He went to the vat and froze. He'd completely forgotten Mrs Wilkins dwelt within. It was early, too early for anyone else to arrive. He relaxed and breathed a sigh of relief. Laboriously, he sieved the glutinous gunk into ingot moulds and set them aside to 'go off'. He raked out the dregs and separated the bones from any muscle or tendons that remained. The football was there, intact but bereft of any flesh and devoid of any hair. Even the eyes that witnessed his assault had dissolved within the feculence. He smashed it with a claw hammer, mixed it with the other chippings and shoved the whole lot into a sack, ready for the bonecrusher.

Stan knocked off and collared Llewellyn on the way out. He was going to decorate, needed some glue and would be more than willing to pay for it.

'Don't be daft!' chortled the Welshman, 'You take what you need. Good of you to ask though, boy, with manners like that, you'll go far. Mark my words, far you will.'

He filled his pockets with a dozen slabs of glue and hurried off to East Street market where he could get what he wanted at a half decent price, even if it was hooky. He guessed five rolls would be enough. A pale, creamy colour with tiny, burgundy diamonds splashed across it. Inoffensive, stylish and not too girly. Girly. Eileen. He fancied surprising her with a present, a token of his affection. He was too embarrassed to buy nylons and didn't know enough about hats to chance one of those either. He didn't even know how big her head was. The last stall but one was shutting up shop. A small bloke with greasy hair and an overcoat one size too big was packing up his wares. Dozens of elegant, cobalt blue bottles of perfume in expensive looking boxes.

'Whassat, mate?' he asked, nodding towards the perfume.

'Foreign, that is mate, all the way from France. It's called 'So-ere dee Pahreese', ladies love it!'

'You what?' asked Stan.

He leaned forward and took a closer look at the label – 'Soir de Paris'. It looked classy.

'How much?' he asked.

'Tell ya what, it's late, I don't wanna carry it, you can do me a favour. Two bob and it's yours. Can't say fairer than that.'

He pocketed the perfume and went straight to the pub. Eileen was at the bar giggling with another girl. She was about the same height, with shoulder length, curly, blonde hair. She wore a black-and-white polka dot dress with a 'v' neck and white collar. Stan saw them and walked over. Eileen grabbed him round the arm.

'Stan, this is Jean. Jean, this is Stan,' she said, beaming. 'We go way back.'

'Ooh, you're alright, ain't ya! Pleased to meet ya, Stan!' said Jean.

Her voice grated on his ears. He grinned, slightly embarrassed.

'Likewise,' he said, trying not to stare at her ample bosom. 'Wanna drink?'

He bought a round and they sat together in the corner.

'What's all this then?' asked Eileen.

'Wallpaper, love. You use it to decorate walls.'

'Ooh, he's a right one, ain't he!' screeched Jean, her leg accidentally deliberately brushed against his.

'Thought I'd do the bedroom, tomorrow like, could do with a freshening up, if you ain't got plans that is.'

Eileen put her drink down and placed her hand on his thigh.

'Why don't you give yourself a break, Stan, stop working so hard, it's all he ever does!' she said, looking at Jean. 'Take yourself off with the lads for a change, go out with your mates.'

Stan laughed.

'Mates? I ain't got no mates! No bother mind, like it

like that.'

'Okay then, that's grand, because… I was thinking of going out with Jean tomorrow, down to Kent for the day.'

'Kent? Garden of England. Sounds nice, love. Something special is it?'

'We're going to see some mates,' said Jean, staring at Stan over her sophisticated schooner of sherry. 'They used be up here but they're all in Marston now.'

'Marston, ay? They WRAFs then or what?' asked Stan.

'S'right, some of them. Couple of pilots too! Be a sort of, reunion, won't it Eileen?'

'Sure it will, be good to see them again. Then I can see you,' she said looking at Stan, 'on Sunday!'

They supped another round. Stan checked his watch, made a pathetic attempt at yawning and fumbled with the rolls of wallpaper. He got up to leave.

'Better get these back while I can still stand!' he joked.

Jean stood up and gave him a peck on the cheek.

'See ya, Stan!' she said, and licked her lips, slowly.

Eileen grabbed his arm.

'I'm coming with you, before she eats you alive.'

Stan walked Eileen to the door and kissed her on the doorstep. She held him tight around the neck, pulled herself up and whispered in his ear. Her breath was warm and moist.

'Can't wait till Sunday,' she whispered.

He dropped the wallpaper. He knew what she meant.

'Nor can I,' he said. 'Nor can I.'

* * *

The conscript was delirious with pain, riddled with fear and far too young to be fighting another man's war.

'I'm gonna help you mate, stay calm! I'm gonna get you sorted!' hollered Stan.

Another shell screamed overhead. He threw himself to the ground and prayed it would keep going. He could hardly hear himself above the boom of artillery fire. He crawled across the dune and shouted again, 'Stay down mate, nearly there!'

The sand stuck to his sweat-ridden brow and lacerated his skin each time he tried to wipe it away. He was drenched with perspiration.

'Where are you?' bellowed the youngster through his tears, 'Stay away from me, stay away!'

Stan crept up beside him. It was then he saw his eyes, then, he understood the anguish and the despair. They were red, bleeding and clotting. He was blind as a bat. He coughed up some crimson phlegm. Stan gasped as someone thumped him in the belly. He looked down to see the bayonet buried in his gut, the young lad's hand clenched tight around the handle. There was no pain, just disbelief, astonishment. He pulled it out and reassured the boy once more that everything would be okay, then slapped him hard across the face and dragged him back to base. He opened his tunic and felt the sticky mess beneath his shirt.

'Think I caught one, Sarge, can't blame him.'

He took some morphine and braced himself for the needle. He winced and grimaced as the surgeon stitched up the ragged gash, boldly, quickly, crudely. He looked over at the lad. He was motionless. Flies buzzed around his eyes.

'Poor sod,' said Stan. 'Poor, bloody sod.'

He woke, wheezing, panting hard. Two empty bottles lay next to him. He didn't remember drinking anything when he returned from the pub. He didn't remember going to bed. He didn't know why he was lying on the floor. He looked down at his stomach and gingerly traced his index finger along the four inch scar. He thought he was going mad.

* * *

A heady bouquet of death and decay wafted from the kitchen as the glue slowly melted in the pan. He added some water, turned down the heat and let it simmer while he stripped the room. By nightfall he'd sized the walls and started papering. He worked through the night, slapped some paint on the woodwork and stopped, only occasionally, for a slug of whisky.

The late winter sun made an effort to brighten the room. Shattered, he sat back to admire his handiwork. The papering was seamless. His mother's double bed seemed happier in his room. Bedside cabinets, each with their own table lamp, straddled the bedstead. The walnut wardrobe nestled snugly in the alcove and the dresser sat beneath the window. He'd even hung a mirror above the mantle. 'Better than the bleedin' Savoy,' he mumbled, and toasted himself with another shot of Teachers. He grabbed forty winks on the couch for fear of ruffling the sheets.

A knock at the door shook him to his senses. It rattled him, made him nervous. He wasn't expecting anyone, unless he'd forgotten. He crouched beneath the window and peered through the net curtains. It was Eileen, dressed in her special frock, clutching a pie dish.

'I made us supper!' she beamed, grinning from ear to ear.

He smiled and kissed her on the lips, apologised for his dishevelled appearance and led her to the kitchen where he poured them both a glass of beer.

'You look radiant,' he said, 'day out obviously did you good, have fun?'

'Aye, it was grand, seeing the girls again and all, especially the Yanks, they're a funny lot, they all look like film stars!'

'Yeah, Groucho and Harpo. Come on, something to show ya.'

They went upstairs and he made her close her eyes before he opened the door.

'Oh Stan, it's gorgeous! You must be worn out!' she said.

'Well, a bit, but not too bad. Took longer to shift the bed than it did to paper the walls!'

'Well, all I can say, Mister, is, if your mother was here, she'd be right proud of you.'

Stan raised the corner of his mouth in a wry smile.

'Oh, don't you worry, love. As long as this house is standing, there'll always be a part of her here. Cheers.'

Eileen sat on the bed. He opened the top drawer of the dresser and took out the box of Soir de Paris.

'Got ya something,' he said, passing it to her, 'French it is.'

'What? But Stan, it's not even my birthday! It's beautiful, thank you!'

'No need, probably full of paraffin.'

She opened the bottle, took a sniff and dabbed some behind her ears.

'No, it's not. It's gorgeous, here, smell.'

She tilted her head toward Stan's and he breathed deeply.

'Nice.'

She turned and kissed him.

'Nicer still.'

She kissed him again and they fell back on the bed. She kicked off her heels, gathered her dress around her waist and sat astride his groin. He ran his hands along the backs of her thighs. They were soft, like cashmere, as smooth as alabaster and comfortingly warm. He reached the edge of her knickers and wondered if her cheeks would feel the same. He stopped, unsure if he should continue and strained to contain himself. Eileen pulled them to one side and a few minutes later it was over. His heart was racing as she snuggled up beside him.

'Pie's burning,' he said.

'So am I,' she replied, and slipped beneath the covers.

Chapter Four

The stench was rank. Her stomach tightened and she retched again. She dropped to her knees and clutched her tummy. The cramps were crippling. She was afraid and, for the first time in her life, she didn't want to be alone. She dressed in a daze and hurried round to Stan's as quick as she could.

The sky hung heavy with the threat of snow. She leaned into the bitter, biting wind which strived to blow her off her feet. She didn't have a scarf, couldn't lay claim to a hat and used her pockets as gloves. By the time she got there she was shivering. Stan opened the door. She was white as a sheet.

'Christ, you look like you've seen a ghost, get in quick!'

She quivered in his arms, he wrapped her in reassurance and placed his palm on her forehead. She was boiling. She raised her eyes to his, like a fawn caught in a snare.

'Don't move,' he said, 'I'm going to get the quack.'

* * *

The surgery was closed. He banged the door till someone answered. It was the receptionist, a battleaxe of a woman who'd spent her entire life scowling at anyone who sneezed.

'Surgery don't open till eleven. Come back in an hour, and if you bang that door again I'll get the law on ya. Now bugger off!'

Stan smiled at her and spoke very quietly.

'Is the doctor here?' he asked. 'I mean, actually here?'

'So what if he is?'

'Go get him. It's my Eileen, something's up.'

'I said come back in an hour, I won't tell…'

Stan stepped forward till he was almost upon her, looked down at her greying hair and whispered.

'Get him. Now. I ain't asking again.'

She left the door ajar and scooted inside. Two minutes later the doctor came out. He breezed by Stan without even looking.

'Come on,' he said, 'where to?'

Eileen was by the fire.

'Is there somewhere we can go?' he asked, looking at Stan.

'Bedroom. Upstairs.'

Fifteen minutes passed. The doctor came down, packed away his stethoscope and spoke bluntly.

'She needs rest. Plenty of it. And something to keep her strength up. Soup.'

'She alright?' asked Stan. 'Is it serious?'

The doctor looked at him disapprovingly.

'I think I can safely say it's not life threatening. Just nature taking its course.'

'Ay?'

'She'll tell you. Now, if you don't mind…'

He paused by the front door, hand on latch, and turned to Stan.

'Married?' he asked.

Stan said nothing.

'Thought not. Oh, by the way, if you threaten my staff again, I'll have you locked up. Good day.'

* * *

'You're an angel,' croaked Eileen, as he entered the room. 'Stan, sit down, I've something to tell you. I…'

'Not now love, you heard what the quack said – rest. Now, you get your head down, I'm nipping up the pub, tell 'em you won't be in. Then I'm going to see old man Llewellyn, see if he'll let me have the day off tomorrow, Monday's always quiet anyway, don't think he'll mind. Back in a jif.'

By the time he returned she was out for the count. She looked tiny in the bed, like the Barnardo's child he never met. He smiled, gently closed the door and left her to sleep.

Downstairs, he cradled a cup of Bovril and dozed off in the armchair. It was dawn when Eileen woke him. Clad only in his dressing gown, she kissed him on the head and tousled his hair. He patted her bottom and offered to make breakfast. She declined, moved away and sat at the table.

'Stan, we need to talk. I've something to tell you.'

'Alright, love, what is it? Everything all right?'

'Yes, everything's, no. I don't know.'

'Well,' he said, chuckling 'either it is, or it ain't! Come on, spit it out!'

'I don't know how to… I mean, I…'

She took a deep breath and blurted it out.

'I'm pregnant! There. Said it. I'm pregnant.'

Silence. He stared blankly into space while she nervously gnawed at her fingernails. His jaw tightened and she prepared herself for the worst as he stood up and tucked his shirt in. He looked at her and grinned.

'Wilkins and Son!' he said, and clapped his hands.

'What?'

'Bloody marvellous!'

'You mean, you don't want me to go?'

'Go? Go? You ain't going nowhere, except to change! Come on, we're going out, we're going to celebrate!'

She cried, then laughed, then ran to hug him. He lifted her up and held her tightly in his arms.

'Right! First thing,' he said, 'rest. No, we're going out. No, first thing, vicar. Need to make an honest woman of you, don't we? No, names! We need to decide on a name! Boy or girl? Boy! Course it's going be a boy. Box room. Upstairs. We can put the cot in there, I'll do it up like…'

'Stan!' cried Eileen. 'Stop it! Stop, for a minute, just stop!'

Stan put her down and lifted her chin with his hand.

'What is it, love? What's up?'

She lowered her head.

'That's not everything,' she said.

'Eh? Well, what else can there be? Blimey, don't tell me it's bleedin' twins!' he joked. 'Still, in for a penny…'

She didn't look up. She held both his hands and squeezed them tight, closed her eyes and whispered.

'It might not be yours.'

He broke away, moved silently to the window and lit a cigarette. She didn't budge, she remained still, motionless, apart from her shoulders which trembled with grief. He turned to look at her. At this elfin beauty, this gorgeous muse, and saw a perfidious wretch swathed in deceit. His eyes narrowed. He stubbed out the fag, stepped behind her and wrapped his arms around her waist, He nuzzled his head in her neck.

'Might, you said. Might not. You don't know, so, no-one need know.'

She turned around.

'What are you saying?' she said.

'Doesn't matter whose it is, I'll still be his dad. I'll still be the one who brings him up.'

'You'd do that?' she wept. 'What did I ever do to deserve you?'

She smiled through glassy eyes.

'I'm not going to go on about it, but the other bloke, if it wasn't me…'

'Before I met you. Just before. Yank. It was silly, I got drunk and one thing… I am so sorry Stan…'

'Shhh. Nuff said. You don't even know if it's his.'

* * *

They sat huddled together, eyes closed, warmed by the fire. She couldn't hear the noises in his head. The shouting and the screaming. She couldn't see the flashing lights, the gaping wounds or the pools of blood. She couldn't smell the vomit or the burning flesh. But she could feel his angst every time his head twitched or his shoulders shook involuntarily. He opened his eyes. It was dark outside.

'Hot bath,' he said. 'That'll help you relax. Hot bath, nice drop of whisky. You'll sleep like a log.'

'Sounds nice,' she whispered.

The windows steamed up, condensation dripped from the taps. He tipped a large dose of Epsom salts into the bath as Eileen watched him from the doorway.

'Good for you, love, the old salts, like. Works wonders.'

'Grand.'

'Here.' He passed her a tumbler of whisky.

'That's rather a large one, isn't it?'

'We're celebrating! Besides, help you sleep. Come on, down the hatch.'

She took the glass, looked into his dark, vacuous eyes and tried to understand the pain he was going through. Tried to look for some kind of light inside. There was nothing. Not even a spark. She raised herself up onto tip-toe and kissed him. He pulled the dressing gown from her shoulders and let it drop to the floor. Even with her gamine figure it was impossible to tell she was with child.

He waved his hand through the water.

'Be careful,' he said, 'might be a bit hot.'

She held him for support and slowly lowered her foot into the steaming bath. It was just about bearable. She lay back. He handed her another Scotch, they clinked glasses and knocked it back. Her face flushed. Waves of consciousness flowed from her body as the heat and alcohol mixed inside her. She felt dizzy, tired. He handed her a third and she pushed it away.

'Oh Christ, I don't think I can take anymore Stan, I don't feel right.'

'It'll help, trust me. Down in one.'

She did as she was told and handed him the empty glass. He moved behind her and massaged her shoulders.

She closed her eyes and softly hummed a tune. He stroked her hair and listened to the bluebirds flying over Dover.

'Stanley Wilkins,' she slurred, 'you're the best man a woman could wish for. Don't know what I'd do if you ever left me.'

'Soppy cow,' he whispered.

She was drowsy. Her body, limp. She mumbled almost incoherently.

'I never meant to hurt you, Stan. I'm not that kind of girl, you know, I don't… sleep around. I'm not like…'

She paused.

'It's alright, love, you can say it.'

'I'm not like your mother.'

He stroked her hair and took a large slug from the bottle.

'That's not quite true though, is it?' he sighed. 'Thing is, you are just like me mother. Why do you have to be just like me mother?'

With one hand atop her head, he shoved her down, hard, sharply, swiftly, surely, till she was under. He held her there. She thrashed like a fish out of water, she flailed her arms in a vain attempt to grab him, the bath, something, anything. She kicked so hard she cut her feet on the taps. Cherry coloured clouds drifted beneath the surface of the water. He looked down at her. At her eyes. Her big, wide eyes, shining like pearlescent stepping stones, filled with fear, tainted with treason. Eventually the bubbles came. Big bubbles that blurted from her mouth and popped on the surface. Then it stopped. Abruptly. There was no more noise, no more splashing. It was calm, as still as a mill pond. He looked at her naked body, as lean and as white as a fillet of fish. 'You stupid, bloody cow,' he said. 'Have to do the living room now.'

* * *

Stan was flummoxed. He hadn't expected to see the quack again so soon. Another ten yards and he'd have been home dry. He forced a smile. The doctor eyed the four bottles of stout dangling from his fingertips and raised an eyebrow.

'Celebrating, are we?' he asked.

'Er, yeah. Well, got cause to now, ain't we,' said Stan.

'And how is young…' he clicked his fingers in the air '…Eileen.'

'Right as rain! All thanks to you, Doc. Like you said, rest, that's all she needed. Goin' to see her later.'

'Going? She's not with you?'

'No, no, she went 'ome, ages ago.'

'Jolly good. Tell her to take it easy on that stuff,' he said, pointing at the bottles. 'Any problems, you know where to find me.'

'Right you are, Doc. Right you are.'

He heaved a sigh of relief and went indoors. The first bottle went down a treat. He opened a second. His left eye twitched uncontrollably. Somebody screamed inside his head. He took a knife from the drawer and went to see Eileen. She was beginning to bloat. 'Not sure if this one'll make it, Sarge.'

He made a single incision in each of her thighs, deep enough to sever the femoral artery, and left her overnight for the blood to drain away. Come the morning he could hardly see her. 'Looks like you've been bathing in tomato juice, love.' He washed and hurried to the yard.

Llewellyn called him over. He was concerned. He slung an arm around his shoulders and asked about Eileen in a caring, fatherly way. It touched Stan, made him feel like a kid again. He felt obliged to confide in him. He shuffled nervously and broke the news gently. 'Expecting!' he said. Llewellyn was beside himself with joy, his baritone voice boomed across the yard.

'Congratulations lad! That's my boy! Glad to see you've got yourself sorted, knew you'd do it, so I did!'

He gave him a hearty whack on the back and the rest of the week off.

'Well, haven't got any cigars, so you may as well get used to looking after the little lady!'

Stan suggested he could perhaps use his time a little more constructively and render the brickwork in the cellar of the house – 'could be a hazard to the little un, just need some lime.' With Llewellyn's blessing, he heaved a couple of sacks on his shoulder and headed on home.

Eileen was waiting for him, her face an ivory island in a sea of cherryade. He pulled the plug, wrapped her in a sheet and carried her down to the cellar where he laid her out like the sacrificial virgin at a pagan ritual. He sprinkled a thick layer of lime in the old tin bath, oiled his mind with scotch and picked up the cleaver. This time he wasn't going to be so fastidious, so neat, or so precise. The cleaver smashed through her ankle and severed her foot. He held it by the heel, brought the cleaver down again and lopped off her toes. He marvelled at how small and ineffectual they were and tossed them, one by one, into the bath.

This little piggy went to market,
this little piggy stayed at home…

Then came the lower legs. He sliced the flesh from the bones and threw that in the tub too. Then her thighs, her soft, milky-white, slender thighs. He stroked them in turn, gave her a smile and severed them at the hip. He sliced through her belly like a side of beef, rolled up his sleeves and reached inside. He fumbled around the mass of blubbery, slippery organs and yanked them from her torso till she was as hollow as a chicken ready for stuffing. Soon there was nothing left. Nothing but her head. Her delicate, porcelain-skinned head. Her eyes were filled with compassion, he knew she understood. He stroked her hair, took another slug of scotch and brought the cleaver down for a final time. The sound of the wireless drifted downstairs.

Last night I went out drinking,
When I come home I give her a beating,
So she catch up the rolling pin
and went to work on me head till she bashed it in.
I lie stone cold dead in the market,
Stone cold dead in the market,
Stone cold dead in the market,
She killed nobody but her husband.

He spread her out in the tub, covered her in lime and left her to cure, just like a gammon joint. Twenty-four hours and she'd be ready for the pot. He cleaned up, turned off the lights and went to bed. It was the first sound night's sleep he'd had in weeks.

The market was heaving, it always was in the morning, everyone wanted the same thing, the pick of the bunch, the cream of the crop, the tastiest, cheapest bargains. He sought out the bloke who sold him the wallpaper before.

The stallholder didn't recognise him, '...don't know you from Adam mate, but if you say you was 'ere before, I believe ya. I'll knock a couple of bob off...' He walked away with half a dozen rolls, white with tiny, fuchsia pink fleur-de-lys across them. He smiled. Eileen would've liked the fancy pattern, the fuchsia pink.

By nightfall the room was stripped. He filled the stock pot and three saucepans with the choicest cuts from the bath, topped them up with water and set them on the hob to simmer. He headed for the pub. He was getting smart, had to think ahead, cover his tracks and put himself above suspicion.

'Alright, Stan?' asked the landlord as he plonked a pint on the counter, 'How's our Eileen then, feeling better?'

'What? You mean she ain't 'ere yet?' said Stan, sounding concerned.

'Nope, thought she was with you.'

'Nope. Thought she'd be 'ere. Now you're getting me worried.'

'Calm down Stan, she's a grown woman, she'll be alright.'

'Yeah, I know. Even so, not like her really is it?'

'Probably still feeling a bit peaky, 'aving a lie down.'

'Yeah, that's it. Probably having a lie down. Still, maybe. I'll pop round hers and check, won't hurt, will it?'

He left. Pulled his collar up against the biting wind and headed for Eileen's. He knocked the door, stepped back and looked up at the windows. A curtain twitched. He knocked again, louder, and eventually the landlady opened the door. He assumed it was the landlady, he'd never met her before.

'Evening,' he said politely, 'I'm Stan, Stanley Wilkins. I've been…'

'I know who are,' she said curtly. 'You're that lad what's been seeing Eileen ain't ya? You better come in 'fore you catch ya death.'

'Thanks. How is she? Feeling better?'

'Dunno love. Don't even think she's here. Hang on, I'll go and check her room, you wait 'ere.'

She thumped up the stairs and disappeared round the landing. He heard her tap the door and call her name, 'Ei-leeen?' The door creaked open. There was a pause, then it slammed shut again.

'Not 'ere,' she yelled, as she made her way back down. 'Must've gone out. You got a message for her?'

'Yes, just tell her I called, would you, please. She knows where to find me.'

'Right you are. 'Ere, you better not be messing her around, lad, or…'

'Quite the opposite. Quite the opposite. Night.'

* * *

Snow began to fall. Light, moist flakes that darted across the street lamps and disappeared into the darkness. He shivered as he got indoors. Eileen was bubbling away. She stank like a dog food factory. 'Just been looking for you,' he said. He threw in some glycerine and let her stew all night.

'Come up a treat, you 'ave,' he mumbled as he stirred her up and sieved her into empty jam jars. He refilled the pans and put a second batch on to simmer. By midday, still in his pyjamas, he'd papered two of the walls. By dusk, bar rearranging the furniture, he'd finished. He dressed and nipped to the pub to see the landlord.

Eileen had not shown up for work. Stan feigned surprise.

'That does it,' he said, 'I'm going to get Plod.'

'Don't be too hasty, Stan,' said the landlord, 'give her a chance. She's probably on the bus as we speak, 'ere, she probably went to see that blonde sort, her mate, tell her the good news.'

Stan rubbed his chin and frowned.

'I dunno, I just… alright. If she ain't back tonight, that's it. And if you see her, tell her I ain't happy. This ain't what I signed up for.'

The landlord laughed. Stan left with a couple of bottles to see him through the night and went back home. He poured off what was left of Eileen and spent the evening erasing all evidence of his culinary skills. He languished in the bath before going to bed.

He shivered as he woke. It was bitterly cold. The garden was coated in a thick, white frost. He padded downstairs, stoked up the fire and made a brew. He gulped it down in an effort to warm up. The cellar was musty and dank and too frigid for flies, despite the appetizing feast festering in the tub. He picked out the bones and smashed them with a hammer until all that remained were hundreds of calcium chips. He swept them into the tub, mixed everything into a nutrient-rich, organic fertiliser and heaved it upstairs. He left it in the garden and went to change. He had to see Plod.

* * *

The desk sergeant was leaning on the counter looking perplexed. He glanced up at Stan, sighed, tapped his pen and went back to his crossword. Stan coughed, politely.

Plod folded his paper in half, took a report form from the tray and spoke lethargically.

'Name?' he asked.

'Eileen. Eileen Doyle.'

'Funny name for a bloke.'

'Not me,' sighed Stan, 'Me Mrs, well nearly. Gone missing, she has.'

'Missing you say? I see. And when was the last time you saw her?'

'Day before yesterday. No, three days ago. It's not like her. She ain't showed for work neither, at the pub.'

'And you're sure she's not off visiting relatives, gone to see a friend?'

'Nope. She would've said.'

'And you've not had a barney? Difference of opinion, perhaps?'

'Nope,' said Stan. 'Nothing like that.'

'Right then. Be quicker if you do this. Fill it out, name, address, description. I'll get someone round to see you as soon as possible.'

'And that's it?'

'That's it. Can't put a search out till we get more details.'

'And in the meantime, I just sit and worry?'

'S'right.'

* * *

Beneath the frost, the soil was moist and crumbly. Stan cursed as he forked it through, the cold had robbed his fingertips of feeling and blistered his palms. He dug a trench the entire length of the bed, tipped in the fertiliser and covered it over. Someone called his name. Or something like it. He froze and listened again. It was faint and came from the street. He leaned over the fence.

'Out back!' he yelled.

A policeman ambled round the corner. A tall, skinny lad who would have looked more at home in the playground than pounding the beat. Stan met him at the gate. His face was blue.

'Mr Wilkins?'

'That's me,' said Stan.

'Mr Stanley Wilkins?'

'Like I said, the same.'

'Constable Porter. I've come about… blimey, you're a state, what ya doin'?'

'Digging for victory,' said Stan, dryly.

'Rather you than me. Wrong time of year to be gardening, ain't it?'

'You obviously ain't a gardener. Soil. Gotta turn it, see, get it ready for planting. Weather like this you gotta let it breathe.'

'Right. If you say so. Now, about this missing person, Eileen Doyle…'

Stan furnished him with the same information he'd written on the form at the station. He spoke quickly, and took satisfaction from watching the young bluebottle struggle to write everything down in his notebook. Ten minutes later they were joined by a detective inspector, an older, wiser copper who asked sensible questions pertaining to her last seen whereabouts, questions that may help track her down, questions that they didn't already have the answers to. He berated the constable for wasting Stan's time. 'Gotta learn I suppose,' he said. He left Stan with words of consolation and told him not to fret too much.

'She'll turn up, sir, don't you worry, nearly always do.'

'Yes,' thought Stan, 'but will she be breathing?'

* * *

The following day, late afternoon, another knock at the door. Stan peeked from behind the curtains. It was the constable again. 'Interfering sod.' He opened the door with a look of excitement and raised his eyebrows.

'Alright?' he said. 'Got some news, then? You found her?'

'Can I come in?' asked the constable.

'If you must.'

Stan didn't like him. Didn't like his attitude. Didn't like the fact some bloke a few years younger than him was acting like his superior. He didn't offer him a seat or a cuppa. He stood in the living room with his arms folded. The constable removed his helmet and clutched it under his arm.

'Funny niff in 'ere, ain't there?' he said.

'Is there? Don't notice it myself. Anyway…'

'Right, sorry. Just a couple of questions, won't take long. You say you walked Eileen home?'

'That's right. Always do.'

'Did you see her go indoors?'

'Can't say I did. Let me think… I watched her walk up the path, she took out her keys, but… no, can't say I saw her go indoors.'

'Thick skinned sort, is she?'

'Eh? What you on about?' asked Stan, his heckles rising.

'Not one to feel the cold. Sir.'

'What you getting at? Course she felt the cold, she's a little thing.'

'Then what did she wear when you walked her home? Only, I couldn't help notice her coat, hanging there, by the door.'

He gestured towards the hallway.

'She's got more than one bleedin' coat!'

'So she left that one here, and wore a different one to go home?'

'Yes. Use your noggin' mate, look, we was courting, stepping out. If you go look in the wardrobe you'll see everything else she left 'ere.'

The constable looked uneasy, he'd driven up a cul-de-sac.

'Erm, that won't be necessary,' he said.

'Right,' said Stan, 'got any more stupid, bloody questions?'

'Sorry. No. I think that's all. Best be off.'

Stan slammed the door behind him and reached for a bottle of stout. He was lucky the nosey copper didn't accept his invitation to look inside the wardrobe. There was nothing of Eileen's anywhere, apart from the stupid, bloody coat.

* * *

'What in God's name possessed you to go back, Porter?' yelled the inspector.

'Dunno, sir,' replied the constable. 'It's just that, well, I read up on him, seems his mum went missing and…'

'His mum took off with her fancy man, she is not missing, she's in bloody Margate! Case closed!'

'Alright, well, the other thing, I noticed, when I went round, was her coat. Her coat was hanging in the hallway.

It was freezing when he walked her home but he claims she wore another one.'

'Then we must take his word for it, that she did,' said the inspector.

He leaned back in his chair and spoke quietly.

'How many coats do you own, Porter?'

'Well, let me see, I've got me overcoat, a mackintosh, that nice tweed… three, I think. Three, sir.'

'Then what's the bloody problem? Listen to me,' said the inspector, 'and listen carefully. Wilkins risked his life for the likes of you, now he's going through the mill cos she's having a baby and he don't know where she is! Leave the detective work to us and keep your bloody nose out. Understand?'

'Sir. Yes, sir! I dunno though, something just don't smell right.'

Chapter Five

Llewellyn offered Stan the paternal guidance he craved and it tore him apart that, in moments of lucidity, he couldn't tell him the truth. He couldn't tell him what he'd been through, what he'd seen or what he'd done. The only person he could ever tell wore a cassock and a collar and he wasn't going to cross that threshold, not if it meant crucifying himself. He bit his lip as Llewellyn dished out the advice again, different story, same words.

'Face it boy, it's not like she's been murdered! She was upset, distraught I dare say, well who wouldn't be? Couldn't face you. Took herself off somewhere she could be alone, with her thoughts like. If she ever did come back mind, and I'm sure she will, I can tell you now, it won't be with a mab. Move on, lad, you've got your whole life ahead of you, it's time to move on.'

* * *

Friday night. Rather than sit on the couch with four bottles of stout, Stan decided a night in the pub would be better suited to lifting his spirits. Two pints down and he was bored. The crowd irritated him. The noise of the piano, as it plinked and plonked its way through endless, banal songs about the war, grated on his ears. He knew it was a long way to Tipperary, his troubles were too large to fit in an old kit bag and mother Kelly's doorstep was nowhere near paradise. He stood to leave when she walked in. Jean. All the fellas looked at her. The girls eyed her with disdain. She was brash, effervescent and had a touch of style. She spotted Stan straight away and headed over.

'Gin and tonic,' she purred, with a lick of the lips. She sat demurely, crossed her legs and allowed the split in her frock to expose as much thigh as possible. Stan blurted out his first question as though it were a little too well rehearsed.

'Heard from Eileen? She been in touch?' he asked.

'Not a word,' she said, 'that's why I'm 'ere, thought you might've heard something. Never mind, she can stand on her own two feet, that one.'

Jean was a year younger than Eileen. They'd been brought up, like sisters, in the same home. Though Eileen left before her, she still returned every evening to check on her 'little sister'. When it was Jean's turn to battle with the outside world, Eileen even found her a job, at Brooke House, 'you know, the looney bin' where she worked till it was bombed in the Blitz. Ever since then, she'd been slopping-out and changing beds at Hackney Hospital. When Eileen decided to move south of the river it hurt her badly, 'like losing me arm, it was, me own flesh and blood.' Stan was taken aback by her display of vulnerability. She wasn't as hard as she made out and, like himself, obviously enjoyed the odd drink to deal with it. By eight o'clock she was merry. By nine, tipsy. Stan reminded her of the time and how long it would take her to get home. Jean reminded him it was Friday night and she'd quite like another gin and tonic.

The streets were deserted. They heard the landlord bolt the doors behind them. She clutched his arm for support.

'Lord knows 'ow I'll get 'ome now,' she said.

Stan squeezed her hand.

'Better come with me, I suppose.'

* * *

The house was warm. He took her coat, hung it in the hallway and pointed to the living room. 'Make yourself at home,' he said, and went to fetch a couple of drinks. She had good posture. He returned to find her sitting cross-legged on the couch, like a debutante, with her back as straight as a ram-rod. Unlike a debutante, she had unbuttoned her frock just enough for Stan to get a good glimpse of her décolletage. He offered her a glass of port and sat beside her. She sipped it, slowly, and looked at him coyly.

'Always said you was a looker, real gent too, ain't ya?'

'I don't think you should be doing this,' he said, 'I mean, I'm with Eileen, she's your best…'

'Shhh…'

She stood up and began to slowly sway her hips, as though she were dancing with herself. Slowly, seductively, she unbuttoned her frock.

'Somes like me nylons,' she said, 'others like me uniform, they says I make 'em feel better, just like a good nurse should.'

Stan's eyes glazed over. He watched her strip but saw nothing. It was night. Uncomfortably warm. He lay perfectly still as erratic bursts of shellfire illuminated a cloudless sky. The nurse bent over him and unbuttoned his sodden shirt. The wound was weeping. He winced as she ripped the gauze from his belly in one, swift action. She dabbed the gash with alcohol and applied a fresh dressing. She was short with dark, curly brown hair. Her arms muscular, her face moulded into a permanent grimace with more hair on her top lip than she was entitled to. His eyes remained closed as she buttoned his shirt. He felt her hands on his belt. She loosened it and unbuttoned his trousers, stealthily, as though she didn't want to wake him. He swallowed hard as her sandpaper hand tugged at him like a pheasant plucking farmer. She straddled his groin and rocked back and forth with short, sharp movements, groaning at every stroke, like a boxer sparring in the gym. He reached out and touched her satsuma-like thighs, pitted and squidgy. She grabbed him by the collar, bit her lip and squeezed him tight. He was done.

'First time love?' she whispered.

Stan smiled, nervously.

'Pathetic. Never mind, son,' she said as she climbed off, 'you'll get the hang of it.'

He was embarrassed and humiliated. Someone called his name. It was Jean, teetering on her heels. She stood before him, completely naked save for her stockings and suspender belt.

'Ta-daa!' she said, hands on hips. ''Ere! Don't you fall asleep on me now, I ain't that bad! Well? Like what ya see?' she teased.

Stan scanned every inch of her body, from her slender legs to her bony hips, from her skinny waist to her ample bosom, from her flawless neck to her pink face. A face tainted with rouge on the lips and a need in the eyes. He stood to catch her as she stumbled forward. She landed on top him. He stroked her hair as she pulled at his trousers.

'I'm a good nurse, me,' she said, 'I can you make you feel better, much better.'

Stan pushed her on to her back. Her eyes lit up, she gasped and grinned as he rammed into her.

'Oi! Not so 'ard!' she yelped.

'Nurses,' he mumbled.

'Ay? What's that you say?'

'You're all the bleedin' same,' he hissed.

'Gently! Stan! You're hurting me!'

She began to cry. Tears rolled down her cheeks. She pulled at his hair, but he didn't flinch.

'You're all the bleedin' same,' he snarled. 'Not a faithful bone in your body.'

'Please, Stan! I'm begging ya! It hurts, get off!'

His placed his hands around her scrawny neck and squeezed, tighter and tighter. Her eyes bulged like pickled eggs. She coughed and choked, desperate to draw a breath. Her fingers clawed at his neck and scratched him till he bled. She kicked and wrestled until, eventually, she could fight no more. Her body went limp. Dead limp. Her head slumped to the side. Stan looked down at her, panting, sweating. He looked down at the nurse. At her hairy top lip and curly, brown hair.

'Boys grow up,' he said.

* * *

The air was damp. He shivered as a chill ran down his spine. The light bulb flickered. He watched a spider scurry across the table. He rolled down her stockings, removed her suspender belt, and stuffed them into his pocket. He looked at her face, her innocent face, her scarlet lips, and her eggy eyes.

'Why'd you do it?' he asked.

The words never left his mouth.

'Look at you, so lovely. What a waste. What a bleedin', terrible waste.'

He bent down, lay his head on her belly and breathed her in.

'Shouldn't have done that, Jean. You don't cross your best mate, ever. What would Eileen say, eh? Shame on you, you had to go and spoil it.'

He stood up, brushed the hair from her forehead and smiled.

'Still. Must get on.'

The cleaver smashed through her wrist. The spider leapt from the table as her hand bounced and clanged into the tin tub. The blood flowed effortlessly from her arm and dripped onto the cold, stone floor.

If you ain't got nobody
Since you gone and lost your head,
Rigor mortis has set in, daddy,
Jack, you dead.
What's the use of havin' muscles
If your life hangs by a thread,
If you ain't got no red corpuscles,
Jack, you dead.

He tapped the blade as he contemplated his next move. He stroked her knee, then brought the knife down, hard. He stopped abruptly and pictured the kitchen. The new kitchen. It was bright and sunny, like a meadow full of rapeseed. She'd have liked that.

Chapter Six

'Right, listen up you lot, you're going to love this. Especially you, Porter.'

Porter stood up, intrigued. It wasn't every day the beat bobbies were briefed by the likes of an inspector.

'Girl gone missing. Our friends in Hackney reckon we might be able to help, want us to give them a hand.'

The room cheered.

'Alright, calm down! Hackney Hospital reported her missing when she didn't show for work, that was a good three or four weeks ago. She lived alone, kept on the straight and narrow but, by all accounts, she was quite a sociable girl. So, why have Hackney come to us? Seems she knew one Eileen Doyle. That's right, as you know, we're still working on that one. Anyway, this girl, Jean Partridge, she grew up with Doyle and apparently they stayed in touch. Word has it she even came this way to visit a few times, but we can't be sure. So, nose to the ground, sniff out anything you can, let's see if we can place her on our patch. That's all.'

* * *

'Something up?' asked the landlord.

'Nope, everything's fine. Half a bitter, please.'

'You sure you should be drinking? Aren't you…'

'Off duty,' said Porter. 'That's me done for the day.'

'Oh, just thought, if you was still in uniform, no matter. Don't see your lot in 'ere much.'

'I'd say that was a good thing, wouldn't you?'

'S'pose.'

'There is one thing.' He paused to take a sip of his drink. 'That Eileen girl, she still ain't showed up, has she?'

The landlord shook his head.

'Nah. Beginning to fear the worst. Why?'

'Don't matter. Trying to find a friend of hers, that all. Blonde sort, short. Name's Jean.'

'Oh, yeah, her. Friend of Eileen's. She was here a while back, month maybe, give or take. Came to see Eileen, as it happens.'

'And?'

'Wasted trip. Never spoke to her but, oops, hold on, it's your lucky day. Ask him, Stan, he had a drink with her.'

Porter turned as Stan walked towards the bar. The landlord gave him a pint.

'Copper's asking about Eileen's mate. Said you had a drink with her.'

Stan turned to Porter.

'You again. What's up?'

'Nothing to do with me, it's the boys in Hackney, they've lost her. Wondered if she came over this way.'

'Oh.'

'Landlord, here, says you had a drink with her.'

'That's right. What do you want to know?'

He told Porter how she'd come looking for Eileen and found him instead. How they'd sat and had a few drinks. And how she'd got so drunk he'd be surprised if she ever made it home. He also told him about their trip down to Kent, to visit the Yanks.

'Maybe you should talk to the coppers down there,' he said, 'maybe they know where she is.'

Porter liked that line of enquiry and made a note to follow it up. He put away his pad and pencil, assured Stan he would he do his best to find them, and left.

'Mug,' thought Stan as he watched him go.

'Lying git,' muttered Porter.

* * *

The following day Porter relayed his findings to the inspector. He stood, like a proud schoolboy, waiting for the applause. The gratitude was minimal. The information might help the boys in Hackney but did nothing to help their case. He ordered him back to normal duties with a warning not to harass Wilkins. Porter had other ideas. He was certain Stan knew more than he was letting on. He was certain he was involved in their disappearance, and he was determined to nail him.

Saturday morning. Six fifty-five. He rapped the door and waited. Seven o'clock. He rapped again. Harder. Louder. Stan opened the door, bleary eyed, and squinted at Porter.

'You mad?' said Stan. 'It's Saturday, it's my bleedin' day off.'

'We never get a day off,' said Porter. 'A policeman is never off duty.'

'Gawd almighty, you'd better come in, it's perishing out.'

He pointed to the couch.

'In there. I'll stick the kettle on.'

Porter removed his helmet, sat down, and noticed the same smell hanging in the air, fainter than before, but still noticeable.

'I've put milk and sugar,' said Stan, handing him a cup.

Rather than mention the unpleasant odour, Porter asked if he was decorating again, it seemed more polite. He threw in a compliment about the living room too, just for good measure. Stan was taken off guard. Porter witnessed a lighter side to his personality, a side which spoke with enthusiasm, a side bereft of the usual bitterness. Stan offered to show him the bedroom and rattled on about his plans for rest of the house. They stopped by the stairs.

'What's this one?' asked Porter, tapping the door gently.

'Cellar. Not good for anything but coal,' replied Stan.

'Mind if I take a look?'

'Suit yourself, but can't see why, ain't going to decorate it. Coppers. Nosey bunch, aren't you.'

Porter laughed politely, opened the door and went downstairs. Stan switched the light on. The single, naked bulb glowed meekly. Porter peered into the gloom, desperate to find something incriminating. There was nothing. Nothing but coal, two large, seemingly discarded stockpots, an old tin bath, broken garden tools and other bits of rubbish. He was out of luck.

'Come on, what you doin' down there?' shouted Stan.

'Coming,' replied Porter.

He turned to climb the stairs and noticed something through the gap in the steps. Small sacks. Half a dozen, piled up off the ground to avoid the damp. He scurried round to take a look and squinted at the bags. Lime.

'What the 'eck does he want lime for?' he asked himself.

Next to them, on the floor, was something even more intriguing. He prodded it with his pencil then carefully picked it up between his thumb and forefinger. He almost shook with excitement. It was a clump of hair. Blonde hair. He hastily shoved it into his pocket.

'See any rats?' asked Stan.

'Rats! If you'd told me that, I wouldn't have...'

'You should know better mate, this is London. Easy to smell a rat round 'ere.'

Porter froze. Nervously, he handed Stan his cup, thanked him for his hospitality and left. He headed straight for the station, as fast as his feet would carry him. Stan, on the other hand, thought nothing of it. He dressed, donned his coat and headed for the shops.

* * *

Porter waited an hour and a half for the inspector to arrive. By the look on his face, he was not a happy man. He had other things on his mind, like his wife's mutton stew which was simmering away at home.

'This had better be good, Constable, I don't take kindly to having my weekend ruined.'

He sat, stony-faced, and listened in silence as Porter described his findings. He sighed and rubbed his eyes.

'Very clever, Porter. So, this is all supposition, based on a hunch? Correct?'

'Well, not entirely, sir, I mean...'

'You any good at sports, Porter? Because if this is a waste of time, you're heading for the high jump. I've got half an hour. Let's go.'

Porter was so keen to impress, he almost ran from the station. He willed the inspector to walk faster. He could almost taste promotion. He didn't expect to be humiliated in front of his suspect. Stan opened the door. His face said it all. He glared at Porter.

'Keep this up and I'll charge you rent. What the bleedin' hell is it now?'

The inspector stepped forward, apologised for the intrusion and swore it would only take a couple of minutes.

'Better come in,' said Stan.

'Something smells good,' said the inspector.

'Sausages. Probably burnt now,' said Stan. 'Wait 'ere while I turn 'em off.'

The inspector stood by the fireplace, folded his arms and rocked back and forth on his toes.

'Like I say, won't take long, Mr Wilkins. Sherlock here, has a couple of questions he'd like to ask you. Go on, Constable, we're all ears.'

Porter was embarrassed. He cleared his throat before speaking.

'Well, it's just that… it's like this… right. Mr Wilkins. Lime. Mr Wilkins, when I called earlier, I couldn't help but notice you have several bags of lime in the cellar. Now, that strikes me as odd. Would you mind telling me, er, us, the inspector and myself, why you have so much lime?'

'Soda,' said Stan.

'I see. I beg your pardon?'

'Soda and Lime. Mix 'em together. Very refreshing.'

The inspector smirked.

'Very funny, if not also, a little odd.'

'Nothing odd about it,' said Stan. 'Damp. The cellar is damp. You use the lime to make… lime mortar. To repoint the brickwork.'

'Repoint the brickwork,' muttered the constable. 'Repoint… alright, more importantly, then, perhaps you can explain, this!'

He pulled the clump of blonde hair from his tunic pocket and held it aloft.

'Whatsat then?' asked Stan. 'Dog hair?'

'No, Mr Wilkins, it's human hair! Blonde, human hair, Mr Wilkins.'

'Very good. You got a head to go with that?'

'This is no laughing matter, Mr Wilkins! Jean Partridge was blonde, and you were the last one to see her alive!'

'How'd you know?'

'Know what?'

'That I was the last one to see her alive. I'd dare say that was virtually impossible, unless she became invisible when she left me.'

'What…'

'Stands to reason don't it? Someone must've seen her, walking to the bus stop, waiting for the bus, riding on the bus, walking home. Gawd blimey, how'd you ever become a copper?'

Porter's face flushed with frustration.

'Point is, Mr Wilkins, the hair! Where do you think I found it?' he said.

'How do I know? Go on, enlighten me.'

'The cellar. Your bloody cellar!'

Stan looked at the inspector then back at Porter.

'You should go back down there,' he said. 'Probably find a lot more, and some black hair too, not to mention a few greys. Me Dad was grey. And me Mum, well, me Mum was blonde, see. Well, sometimes.'

'I think we've heard enough,' said the inspector.

He stepped forward, shook Stan by the hand and replaced his helmet.

'Sorry for wasting your time, Mr Wilkins. And sorry about your sausages.'

'No bother,' said Stan. 'I'll see you out.'

The inspector put his hand on Porter's shoulder as they walked down the garden path.

'Ever heard of Point Duty, Constable?' he said.

Chapter Seven

The house was a tip. Wispy cobwebs fluttered in the doorway. The curtains remained closed. Feathery balls of dust blew along the hall, discarded plates lay amongst the empty beer bottles in the kitchen sink. Outside it was 21°F, the sun was low and he was late. He rose, still wearing the jacket he'd put on over his pyjamas and the scarf he'd wrapped around his head. He dressed quickly, brushed his teeth and winced as the ice cold water shocked his gums. He trudged through the snow, his feet like anvils. Llewellyn was waiting for him as he entered the yard.

'Third time this week, lad. I'm disappointed,' he said.

Stan said nothing. His head jerked. The tic in his face had become worse.

'Look at you, you're a state, haven't even shaved and, oh God, you smell like a brewery.'

Stan studied his boots. They didn't shine like they used to. He was embarrassed and angry, with himself. Llewellyn shook his head and spoke quietly.

'What on earth's happened, lad? Things catching up with you? Want to talk about it?'

'No, ta, Mr Llewellyn. Just out of sorts, that's all. Be right as rain soon enough.'

'You sure? You eating properly? Tell you what, why don't you come to my house tonight…'

'Really, I'm alright Thanks, all the same.'

'Very well, then. Last chance. Tomorrow. Be here, ready and sober. Now, go home and get cleaned up, and get some rest, look like you could do with it. Off you go.'

* * *

Home. The prospect of bouncing off the walls depressed him. He took himself down to the canal instead where he shivered as he stared at the icy, white waterway and smoked half a dozen fags till the pub opened. The Dun Cow. He ordered a pint and a whisky chaser, sat facing the wall and read a discarded copy of the Daily Mirror. Three pints down and his 'kill or cure' was hanging in the balance. The lunchtime mob unsettled him. Their cheery banter filled him with loathing. He felt agoraphobic. He stood to leave. A smartly dressed man with pock-marked skin and a broken nose caught his eye as he left.

'Oi, geezer, if you need somewhere to kip tonight, the Sally Army's just around the corner. They'll look after ya,' he said.

The words stopped him in his tracks. He looked past the spiv at his reflection and struggled to recognise the vagrant staring back. It turned his stomach. He fled the pub and walked home briskly, cursing every time he slipped on the ice. By the time he reached the front door he was out of breath. He boiled a kettle of water and filled the basin. He regarded his ashen face with disdain. He could hear the blade scrape across his skin as he shaved off the tendrils of complacency. The geyser gurgled and spluttered as it coughed water from the taps. It was tepid, barely four inches deep and turned black as he washed.

Dressed in dignity, he looked in the mirror and welcomed back the man who used to live there. He lit a fire, cleared the kitchen and fried up some liver and onions. Half drunk, the smell almost made him puke. He forced it down, it was the first proper meal he'd eaten in a week. He belched, satisfied, and smiled. All he needed was something to wash it down with. He rinsed the teapot, put the kettle on the hob and changed his mind. The off-licence was a better idea.

* * *

It was just after eleven when Llewellyn rapped the door. Stan stood there in his vest, bleary eyed and swayed gently, like a leaf about to fall in the autumn breeze.

'Sorry it's come to this, lad, but I've got no choice,' he said.

He handed Stan an envelope, his severance pay, and took the keys to the yard. 'Come see me when you're straight, boy. I'll find something for you.'

He walked away, despondent at the way his surrogate son had turned out.

Stan kissed his pay packet, shut the door and went back to bed.

* * *

A dust storm gathered. Visibility dropped to a few hundred yards. The order came to move. One by one, they leapt from the trench. Surrounded by the rumble of tanks, they advanced, cautiously, into the unknown. The grit and the sand stuck to his raw, blistered, sun-burned legs. He stopped as the dust clouds spat a Panzer towards him. It scurried along, like a furious beetle scavenging for food. The turret swayed to the left, and then to the right, then stopped as it recognised him. He prayed as only prey know how. A Crusader stopped it with a single shell. Acrid smoke, as black as pitch, billowed from its belly. A hatch flew open. He charged towards it, bayonet fixed and screamed for all he was worth. Two hands emerged, followed by a head, the head of a teenager, a fresh-faced youngster barely old enough to shave.

'Nicht schiessen! Nicht schiessen!' it yelled.

Stan waved his rifle and beckoned him down. He clambered out of the hatch and stood on the tank. His hands tried to touch the sky. His watery eyes locked on Stan's. He was unarmed. A bullet ripped the cheek from his face and sent him spinning to the ground in a crazed pirouette. The second silenced him before he could scream. Stan stared in disbelief. He turned to his left. A soldier stood, grinning. He wore the same uniform as Stan, carried the same rifle, and fought for the same country, but at the moment, Stan realised they were on different sides. He walked over to the boy, knelt down and closed his pleading eyes.

'Murder,' said Stan. 'Plain and simple. Murder.'

It was almost five when he woke, parched and shivering. The image of the dead lad's face hung in his mind. He wanted to cry but swallowed hard. He wanted to scream but kept his mouth shut. He wanted a drink. He dressed without washing, turned his collar up against the cold and headed out.

His mind was addled. He couldn't concentrate. He mumbled to himself as he crunched his way through the snow and headed for the pub. He walked right past it. He kept walking, cursing and twitching, till he reached the canal. Why? It rankled him. It made him angry. Why was he back at the canal? He watched a mallard hit the ice and skid, uncontrollably, before coming to rest a few yards further down. He felt compelled to join it. Unsure if it would bear his weight, he gingerly stabbed the surface of the ice with the heel of his boot. He shuffled, cautiously, towards the duck. Someone shouted from the bank. It startled him. He turned to see who it was, slipped and landed on his knees.

'Get off the ice, you bloody fool! Do you know how deep that canal is?'

He heard a crack. Slowly, he tried to stand. The ice ruptured and suddenly, he plunged, waist deep, into the frigid water. He clawed desperately at the frozen crust, hauled himself out and slithered snake-like back to the bank.

'You should know better, a grown man like you! What on earth were you thinking? You trying to kill yourself or what?'

He stood to face her and quivered as the wind pulled tears down his cheeks. She was short with piercing, blue eyes and wore a look of disdain over an otherwise plain face.

'Love a duck,' he said, 'you must be an angel.'

'I beg your pardon?'

'You saved me. If I'd gone any further…'

She noticed the stubble on his chin, the pain in his eyes. She smiled.

'You poor thing,' she said.

She raised her hand and stroked his cheek.

'The answer's not out there, you know. There are people who can help you, I can help you.'

Stan was bewildered, mesmerised by her eyes.

'No, you've got it wrong,' he laughed 'I wasn't trying to…'

'Of course you weren't. Now, come on, you're coming with me, you need to dry off before you catch your death.'

He smiled.

'So, you're not an angel?'

'Can you see any bloody wings?'

* * *

They walked to her house on Henshaw Street, just a couple of minutes' walk from his old school, The Paragon. Eloquent, well-spoken and forthright, she offered him tea with a splash of brandy.

'Good for shock,' she said. 'And believe me, you are in a state of shock.'

'Bloody right,' he said, and winked. 'Thanks, you didn't have to.'

'Yes I did. I feel responsible. If I hadn't yelled like an interfering old busy-body, you wouldn't have fallen.'

'Maybe. Maybe I've fallen already.'

'Well, the Salvation Army are very good at picking people up.'

'You're not one of… you know… a tambourine basher?'

She looked surprised, unsure if it was an insult or a compliment, then laughed.

'No, I most certainly am not,' she said with a smile. 'But I do feel duty-bound to help where I can.'

She paused.

'I like you,' she said. 'You're cheeky.'

Stan cradled the cup in both hands and smirked.

'You remind me of someone,' he said. 'Teacher of mine, at the Paragon. Good 'un she was. One of the best.'

The woman raised her eyebrows, intrigued.

'The Paragon? Who, if you don't mind me asking… what was her name?'

'Chadwick. Mrs Chadwick.'

'Well, of all the… really! I can't believe it. How wonderfully small this great, big, world is.'

'Eh? Sorry, don't follow.'

'I'm Florence. Florence Chadwick. You were taught by my mother!'

'Blimey!' said Stan 'Who'd have thought! Hold up, you must've been at school same time as me.'

'I'm sure I was, but I wasn't educated here. Benenden. I was a boarder.'

'Oh. So, what do you do, then, if you don't mind me…?'

'Teacher, at the Paragon!'

'Well, blow me down! Look at me, forgetting my manners.'

He held out his hand.

'Stan,' he said. 'Stanley Wilkins.'

'It's a pleasure, Stanley,' she replied, blushing ever so slightly.

'Well, I really should be… taken up enough of your time. Thanks for the tea.'

He turned to leave.

''Ere, I don't suppose you fancy…'

Her cheeks reddened even more.

'I don't think so,' she interrupted. 'But thank you for the invitation.'

* * *

Florence. Florence Nightingale. She sounded like one, thought Stan, with that plum in her mouth. She was a looker, too. Plain, yes, but unattractive, certainly not. There was something about her. Something about those eyes. He felt energised. Refreshed. He tore home with renewed vigour, bathed and shaved and dressed in his best suit. He decided to try again. 'If at first, you don't succeed, Stan.' It was dusk when he reached her house. He rapped the door, lightly, and took a step back. She hardly recognised him.

'Gosh, you look quite diff… did you forget something?'

'In a manner of speaking,' he said. 'How about that drink?'

She raised a hand to cover the smile she couldn't repress.

'I'll fetch my coat.'

* * *

Miss Chadwick sipped a brandy and ginger and listened intently as Stan regaled her with mournful tales of carnage and bloodshed, lost loves and his mother's moonlight flit to Margate. She was enthralled yet saddened by his honesty, his subdued demeanour and his obvious loneliness.

'Should've been sectioned, me. Easier all round.'

She berated him for being so self-deprecating.

'Sorry, barrel of laughs, eh? What about you? You're too young to be a spinster, and far too pretty to be single.'

She giggled and shuffled a little closer to him. The school was her life. The children. Nurturing them, watching them grow.

'Knowledge,' she said, 'is the key to every door, and I believe every child should have a key.'

'You're proper clever, you are,' said Stan. 'It's admirable, that, what you do. It's a virtue. You, Miss Chadwick, are a paragon of virtue!'

She laughed, loudly.

'This is nice,' she said, looking at Stan. 'I don't get out much these days, well, not as much as I'd like to.'

'What? Lovely girl like you? Why's that?'

'My fault really, that and too much work. I seem to spend more time marking books than I do socialising. But I don't mind, really. I enjoy my own company. I like to read. Friends can be, somewhat, fickle, don't you find?'

'Oh, I do find,' he jested. 'In fact, I finds them so fickle, I like to keep mine to a minimum.'

'And how many is your minimum?'

'None.'

She laughed, like a donkey. Stan went to the bar. She checked her lipstick while his back was turned.

'Been thinking,' he said, 'I'd like to, er, take to take you out, proper like, we could…'

'How wonderful! When? I'd like that. Yes, I think I'd like that a lot. We could go to the British Museum, or the National Gallery.'

'Blimey, I was thinking more of The Dun Cow. Ain't never been to a museum. Or a gallery, come to think of it.'

'Then it's time you did! That's settled then, Saturday. Agreed?'

'Alright, you're on! Never know, might learn something.'

* * *

They left. A lone figure, lean and lanky, and slightly the worse for wear, followed them out. He tailed them at a distance as they walked, arm in arm, back to her house. Stan politely said goodnight to Miss Florence Chadwick. She curtsied, grinned and went indoors, where she promptly danced around the lounge, grinning like the Cheshire Cat. She couldn't recall the last time she'd been asked out. She couldn't recall the last time she'd been out. She raced upstairs and rummaged through her wardrobe, wondering what to wear on their date.

Meanwhile, Stan sauntered home at a leisurely pace. He wondered where the National Gallery was. He wondered what was in it. He wondered if they'd let him in. More importantly, he wondered what it would be like to kiss a toff. Then he wondered how he'd pay for it. Llewellyn. He'd have to see Llewellyn, on bended knee. A cat screeched as he went inside. A lanky shadow slinked down the street.

* * *

The weather showed no signs of abating. Still, the snow fell; still, the wind blew. A line of women queued stoically for bread. He arrived at the yard. An officious looking jobsworth clad in brown overalls barred his entry. He looked at Stan, licked the end of his stubby pencil and studied his clipboard.

'Name?' he asked, in a nasal tone.

'Eh?' said Stan.

'Name? It's only for a week, mind. Now, name?'

'Don't know what you mean, mate. I used to work 'ere? I've come to see Llewellyn?'

'Oh,' sighed The Overalls. 'You haven't heard then?'

'Heard? Heard what?'

'Dead.'

'What?'

'He's passed away. Last week. Keeled over, at home. Heart attack.'

'No! Bloody hell! No, I mean, oh Christ! But… I…'

He paced up and down, three strides forward, three strides back, confused, addled, lost. He reached for a fag, took a single puff and threw it away.

'What… what's all this then?' he asked, waving his arm. 'What's going on?'

'End of the road, son. Selling it off. Be her pension. The wife's, that is.'

'So, that's it? No-one's taking over the…? That's it? That's bloody it?'

'Fraid so. Now, don't shoot the messenger, you want the work or not?'

'But what about their jobs? Them in there? What's going to happen to them?'

'No idea, sir. Now, like I say, do you want the work or not?'

'What? Yeah. Yes. Thanks, yes I want the work.'

'Tomorrow morning. Seven o'clock sharp. Name?'

* * *

Seven o'clock, Friday morning. Stan arrived at the yard. It was quiet. He watched a bloke carry lengths of two by four, one at a time, from the timber store to the gates. No sense of urgency, no sense of purpose. It infuriated him. He wanted to kick him up the backside, just like

Llewellyn would have done, and tell him to pull his finger out. The Overalls called to him from the office.

'Stanley Wilkins!'

'Yes, chief. What's up?'

'Morning, Mr Wilkins. Now, you used to work here, so you know where everything is, correct?'

'That is, correct.'

'Good, in that case, can you make a start in the workshop, please. Tools. Anything and everything. Should raise quite a bit. If you could bring them here, we'll sort them later.'

'Right you are,' said Stan. 'Leave it to me.'

He strolled across the yard, passing the boiler room on the way. The door was ajar. He heard voices. A chill ran up his spine. He remembered the vat. There was something bad about the vat. What was it? Was it something he'd read? Or heard? He peered in. A long, lean shadow crept across the floor and up the wall.

'…and that's it? Glue?' asked Porter.

'S'right, sir. Just glue. Go for scrap now, this will, once it's cleaned out, mind.'

'Thanks. Won't keep you. I'll be off.'

He almost bumped into Stan as he left.

'Mr Wilkins! How, er, nice to…'

'You're like a bloody rash, you are. What you doing, poking around 'ere?'

'Just routine enqu…'

'Routine my arse! Scarper, go on, do one, or I'll do you for harassment.'

'Mr Wilkins, I…'

'I ain't telling you again, Constable…'

'Sergeant, if you don't mind.'

'I don't know what your game is, Porter, but you better...'

'My game, Mr Wilkins, is finding the truth, and by hook or by crook, I'll find it. I'm watching you!'

Stan cursed and headed for the workshop. He had more important things to worry about. By five o'clock his task was done. He'd cleaned the hand tools and neatly sorted them into separate boxes: chisels, planes, hacksaws, tenon saws, coping saws, screwdrivers, hammers, drills, the lot. Overalls was impressed and handed Stan his cash.

'You've a good, tidy mind, Mr Wilkins. Quick too. Would you be interested in something a little more permanent, after this?' he asked.

'I think I would be, ta,' said Stan.

He pointed to the door, to the sign that read 'Office'.

'Mind if I take that?'

'All yours. See you Monday.'

* * *

Florence was waiting on the doorstep. Dressed in a grey, woollen two-piece suit and burgundy beret, she oozed class. Her cheeks glowed, her eyes sparkled like sapphires in the low winter sun. Stan grinned like a fool.

'Sorry I'm late, miss!' he quipped.

She hee-hawed and offered him her arm.

'Forget the National,' she said, 'too stuffy, I've found something much more exciting!'

'More exciting than the National? You're kidding me! Where to, then?'

'Whitechapel.'

'Nice pubs there.'

'The Whitechapel Gallery.'

'Oh.'

* * *

Stern-faced individuals cricked their necks as they studied the exhibits. They looked perplexed but said nothing. It was quieter than a library, as sombre as a church. They looked at paintings, models of buildings, handwritten essays and the odd chair. Stan sighed.

'What's this again?' he whispered.

'Czechoslovakian Modern Art,' she replied, pointing to a painting. 'That's by Konicek. He started the movement with Hofman.'

'Right. So, why is it 'ere, not in Czechoslovakia?'

'So we can see it. And learn from it.'

'And the chair. What's so special about the chair?'

Florence took him to one side and tried to explain.

'Where does a chair come from, Stan?'

'Shop. Seen 'em. On the high street.'

'No. It comes from someone's head. Someone has to design the chair. They have to sketch it out. Decide on the shape, how many legs it will have, how tall it will be, how long it will be. What it will be made of. Then, they have to work out, how, it will be made. Then, they have to make it.'

'Blimey. Never thought of it like that. You just, sort of, take it for granted, don't you? Like they've always been there.'

'Why don't you try? Later? We'll sit down with a pencil and paper and design a chair, together.'

Stan laughed.

'Me? I wouldn't know how… I mean, I don't…'

'Coward!' she smirked.

'Alright! You're…' Something caught his eye and he paused. 'You're on!'

'What is it? What's the matter?' asked Florence, slightly perturbed.

'Nothing. Just thought I saw someone.'

'Someone you know?'

'Sort of. From the yard. Must be mistaken, he wouldn't be up this neck of the woods anyway. Come on! Let's have a drink before we go!'

She clutched his arm as they made their way towards The Blind Beggar. Porter followed discreetly.

* * *

She watched him as she peeled potatoes. He was lost in another world. He bit his tongue and murmured loudly as he scrawled picture, after picture, after picture, totally engrossed, like a five year old swathed in innocence. With every sketch came another improvement, another tweak, another adjustment to 'The Wilkins Recliner', as he called it. Except it didn't recline. Satisfied he could do no more, he lay down his pencil and studied the final sketch with a satisfied look of accomplishment. Florence wandered over. He became flustered and embarrassed and began turning the pages face down.

'Let me see!' she insisted.

Reluctantly, he sat back and grimaced as she turned each page over. She said nothing, but lowered herself into the seat next to his and scrutinised each sketch in detail. Each one was annotated with rough dimensions, methods of fixing, various materials and possible finishes. She frowned.

'I knew this was stupid!' he said, and stood to leave. 'Feel like a right fool! Should never have…'

'Stan! Sit!' barked Florence. 'Sit! Now, where did you learn to draw? You said you couldn't.'

'Can't. Well, never tried. Didn't know…'

'Balderdash. You draw very well. And where did you learn all this, all this mortice and tenon, three quarter business?'

'Well, Llewellyn. The yard, you know. It's rubbish ain't it? You're just being nice.'

'It's wonderful!' she whispered.

'What?'

'It's wonderful, you silly man! Wonderful and brilliant!'

She leaned over, grabbed his face in both hands, and kissed him on the lips. He was stunned, pleasantly stunned, and smiled. He hadn't expected the first kiss to come as such a surprise.

'Blimey!' he said. 'What was that for?'

'You're a genius! A very talented genius!'

'Really? You're not…'

'No, I am not! I think we've found your calling, young man! I've never seen a chair like this, and I've never met anyone who could make it! You're simply brilliant!'

'Really?'

'And stop saying "really". We must celebrate! Come on, forget Potato Pete, pub and a fish supper! We can talk about how we're going to make these properly!'

That night Stan waltzed home, drunk with excitement, head swimming with ideas. He wanted Miss Chadwick to help him bring his fanciful dreams within the realms of reality. He wanted to pick her up and squeeze the life out of her. He wanted to hold on to her. He paused, key in lock, and turned at the sound of footsteps, clacking quickly along the street. A willowy figure faded into the night.

* * *

Florence removed the pink curlers from her chestnut locks, laced up her no-nonsense boots and trudged her way through the icy sludge to Stan's. He took her coat, gave her a hug and a kiss and scuttled back to the kitchen. She followed, slowly, intrigued by his behaviour. The fire was roaring. He was back at the table, surrounded by mountains of paper daubed with scribbles. He'd scrawled on anything to hand: empty fag packets, envelopes, even the margin of the newspaper.

'Give that a stir, would you love,' he said with a grin and pointed to a pan of stew bubbling on the hob.

'Stanley Wilkins, what are you doing?' she asked.

'Cooking. Oh, this? Ideas! Loads of 'em! They won't stop coming!'

She sifted through the papers and beamed with pride. 'The Wilkins Recliner' had been joined by 'The Wilkins Diner,' 'The Wilkins Collapsible Occasional Table' and 'The Wilkins Revolutionary Folding Step Stool Mark I'. He spoke without looking up.

'Could do with a brew, been at it all night.'

'All night!' she exclaimed. 'Are you mad?'

'Probably. Couldn't sleep, me head was spinning.'

'You, are remarkable!' she said. 'Now, come on, time for a break. I'll put the kettle on and we'll sit awhile. I've brought something for you.'

'For me? Whatsat then?'

He stood, gave her a hug like a grizzly and kissed her on the forehead. She giggled and nestled into his chest.

'You'll see. Come on.'

They sat on the couch. Stan slurped his tea. She tutted.

'Would you like a straw?' she asked.

'Sorry.'

'Here, I think you'll enjoy this.'

She handed him a small parcel wrapped in brown paper, tied with string, about the size of a paperback. He opened it carefully.

'Like Christmas!' he enthused, and read the cover out loud.

'*The Wanderings of Oisin and Other Poems.* Poems? Poems? It's a book of bleedin' poems!'

'How very observant of you, Stanley,' smirked Florence.

'But I don't read poems!'

'Why not?'

'Well, they're for, you know, nancies, queer folk, sissies, like…'

'Does he look like a nancy to you?' she asked, pointing to a picture of Yeats on the back cover.

'Well, no, s'pose not.'

'Suppose not, indeed! Not only is he all man, all Irish, I dare say he could bloody well drink you under the table too!'

'Really?'

'There you go again, yes, really!'

'Hmm. Better take a look then. Later. When I've shifted all the furniture from me head.'

* * *

The wireless crackled softly in the background. Arthur Askey joked with his playmates. Stan took her hand, her small, delicate hand, and held it gently.

'What…' he asked, 'What do you see in me, Flo?'

'Not sure I understand, Stanley. What exactly do you mean?'

'Well, you, Flo, you're clever. You're clever and smart, you've got manners, you're well educated, but me, I'm…'

'You're the same! You're smart too, and you've excellent manners. I've just read a little more, that's all.'

'Even so, you should be with someone better than me, someone with a decent job, in the bank or something. Someone who talks nice.'

'Utter tosh!' she said. 'I wouldn't dream of it.'

'You've changed me, you know that? You really have. Feel like I'm going somewhere. Feel like, oh I don't know, like, like spring, when everything's about to grow.'

'Now you're sounding like a poet! Good for you, Stanley! Good for you!'

She grabbed his face and planted a kiss on his lips. He reciprocated and pulled her close. They sat in a huddle, in silence, till nightfall.

* * *

Stan walked her home, saw her safely indoors and returned to his fading fire. He pokered the dying embers, took the book from the table and sat with a sigh. He studied the picture of W.B. Yeats. Bespectacled, studious, professor-like. A thick mop of hair and a pallid complexion. Definitely Irish. He cleared his throat and opened the book at random at 'The Stolen Child':

Where dips the rocky highland
Of Sleuth Wood in the lake,
There lies a leafy island
Where flapping herons wake
The drowsy water rats;
There we've hid our faery vats,
Full of berrys

And of reddest stolen cherries.

'Faery vats? Flippin' barking,' he muttered and closed the book. He went to the kitchen, washed the dishes and poured himself a large whisky. He knocked it back, poured another and stared at Yeats.

'Alright, once more,' he said.

Away with us he's going,
The solemn-eyed -
He'll hear no more the lowing
Of the calves on the warm hillside
Or the kettle on the hob
Sing peace into his breast,
Or see the brown mice bob
Round and round the oatmeal chest
For he comes the human child
To the waters and the wild
With a faery, hand in hand
From a world more full of weeping than he can understand.

A single tear hit the page. Then another, and another.

'Bleedin' poems,' he sniffed.

* * *

It fell from the sky like a lead balloon, silhouetted by the midday sun. He trapped it beneath his right foot and yelled as a boot cracked hard against his shin and scraped the flesh to the bone. He fell, screaming, as the sand buried itself in the gash. 'Foul play, ref!' he yelled, but there was no ref to adjudicate. He got up and gave chase. The tackle was rough, but, as with all things in love and war, fair. His opponent went down in similar fashion and only fifteen yards of clear, open space lay between him and the goalie. His foot hit the ball like a piledriver. It flew, straight and true, towards the keeper and hit him square between the eyes. He went down like a sack of potatoes.

Stan woke, laughing out loud, still wondering how he'd failed to score. He dressed quickly with plans afoot to surprise Florence with something by way of a thank you. He nipped across to Petticoat Lane. It was heaving with the usual traders peddling their Woodbines and 'imported' perfume. An old man, wearing a Homburg and thick, woollen topcoat, was perched on a fishing stool on the kerb. He didn't have a stall or a barrow, just a suitcase tucked between his legs. Stan watched as the man scrutinised a ring through a loupe. He looked up, suddenly, as if startled, and stared straight at Stan. He smiled, gently, and his face erupted in a sea of wrinkles. Stan walked over and knelt beside him. The old boy showed him the ring.

'A thing of beauty,' he croaked, in an accent made of goulash and Bull's Blood, 'should be treated with respect.'

Stan said nothing but nodded his head, infatuated with the sage.

'You, have something beautiful,' he continued. 'Something precious. I can tell.'

'Eh? Don't know what…' mumbled Stan.

'Don't be embarrassed by love, young man. It will keep you alive.'

'Florence,' whispered Stan. 'Her name's Florence.'

'Florence. Florence. One that blossoms.'

'Eh?'

'That's what it means. Florence means one that blossoms.'

'Well I never. She does, too. She's like a flower…'

'Delicate. Fragile. Inspirational?'

'Inspirational. Yeah. Definitely.'

'I have something. Look.'

The old boy opened the case and rummaged around beneath the lining. He brought out a box. A small, black box with a gold rim. He opened it, carefully. Cradled on a bed of velvet was a gold crucifix, not even an inch long, and buried in the middle was a single, tiny stone. A white stone.

'Topaz,' he said. 'Silver Topaz. To keep the fire within.'

'It's beautiful,' said Stan, too scared to touch it. 'How much?'

The old man looked at Stan, his glassy eyes bore into him. Seconds passed.

'It has no price,' he said. 'You have paid for it already.'

'Eh? How's that?'

'Your eyes tell me what your tongue will not.'

He placed it in Stan's palm and closed his hand around it.

'Take it,' he said. 'Take it and remember, a flower is easily crushed. Water it well and give it room to grow. I must go.'

Seconds later, he was lost to the crowd. Stan stood, befuddled. He opened the box. The stone glinted, briefly, in the sunlight. He swallowed hard and headed back to the yard.

* * *

Another flurry of snow drifted, lazily, from the night sky and left a dusting of sugar across his shoulders. He stamped his feet as Florence, wrapped in her housecoat, ushered him inside. They kissed, softly, and went through to the dining room where she'd been sewing at the table.

'This make do and mend lark is all very well, Stanley, but I'm running out of things to mend! Join me in a gin?' she said.

'Don't mind if I do, unless…'

'Wait there! I've a bottle of stout in the cupboard, you'd prefer that.'

'Ta. You know something, Flo? You've been good to me, really, taught me a lot you have.'

'Don't be daft, Stanley, I've simply brought it out of you, it was there all along. Just had to find it, that's all.'

'Well, you found it then. What I'm trying to say is, well… it, you mean a lot to me, more than anything, and I wanted you to know. Got you this.'

He pulled the small, black box from his pocket and handed it to her. It was wrapped in a piece of lined paper.

'Why, Stanley! You shouldn't have, you silly… whatever could it be?'

She unwrapped it.

'You've written on it, are these notes for your…'

She stopped mid-sentence as she read the script, written in his finest hand.

Amidst the grey and ashen 'scape
There grows a bloom
That bears the weight
Of heavy dew
and tears,
of courage
and my fears.

She sobbed, quietly. Stan gave her a hanky. He felt awkward, unsure if he should hold her or leave her.

'It's not that bad, is it?' he quipped.

'It's the most beautiful thing I've ever read,' she whimpered. 'Simply beautiful.'

'Well, it ain't as good as the Irish bloke, I know but I done me…'

'It's every bit as good, Stanley Wilkins. Now, what's this?'

She opened the box and gasped.

'Exquisite!' she sighed, as the tears flowed again. 'I don't know what to say. Look at me, I'm acting like a fool, what must you think of me.'

'You know exactly what I think of you. Here, turn around, I'll help you put it on.'

He fastened the clasp. She closed her eyes and sighed as he tenderly stroked her neck.

Chapter Eight

The yard was deserted. A pigeon cooed from the garret above the workshop. A Bedford stood idle, laden with the last load of scrap. Grains of hope blew across the gritted cobbles. He looked to the sky and saw Llewellyn in a puffy, cuddly cloud, smiled and walked forlornly to the office. He let himself in.

'No point in knocking,' he said.

'Quite alright,' said The Overalls. 'Fancy a cuppa?'

'Ta, very much. Never seen this place so desolate. It's creepy.'

'Anywhere without a soul is creepy, Stan.'

'You're not kidding. So, last day. What needs done?'

'Not much. Drink your tea first. General tidy up is all. Sweeping and binning anything you find on the truck. Leave it neat and tidy, like, for the new folk. We should be out by lunch.'

'Right you are. I'll get on.'

* * *

Twelve-thirty and he was done. The Overalls shook his hand, gave him his pay and handed him a business card.

'Be sure to call, Stan. Could use a few like you,' he said.

'You sound like old man Llewellyn. He said the same thing.'

'Good judge of character then, wasn't he? Speaking of Llewellyn, I have this, for his widow.'

He held up a large brown envelope.

'Some valuables, few knick-knacks. Would you like to drop it round?'

'Rather not,' said Stan, 'if you don't mind, that is. Just feels a bit, funny, you know?'

'Say no more. Good luck Stan, and remember, stay in touch.'

After The Overalls left, Stan ambled up the street, stuffed the cash in his pocket and tossed the pay packet to the kerb. Porter followed and cackled as he picked it up.

'Gotcha!' he whispered to himself.

* * *

Mrs Llewellyn thanked The Overalls for his trouble, sat at the table and tipped the contents of the envelope before her. She counted out the princely sum of six shillings and four pence in loose change and smiled wistfully as she set aside his mother-of-pearl tie clip and the gold-tipped fountain pen she'd bought him for his fiftieth birthday. The wedding band was something she didn't recognise. It was plain and simple and bore an inscription on the inside. 'Gladys. Eternally yours. My love, always. 1919'. 'Well I never…' she muttered, 'we don't know anyone called Gladys.'

'Someone might have lost it. It's a valuable thing, a wedding ring,' she said to the Duty Officer.

'Quite right, madam. You did the right thing, bringing it here. If someone's looking for it, they'll come calling sooner or later,' he replied.

He sealed it in a bag, wrote the date on the front and tossed it in the 'Lost Property' box.

* * *

Stan bought a bunch of flowers, nothing special, just a few carnations, and presented them to Florence with a flourish. She hee-hawed and kissed him on the lips.

'Come on,' he said. 'I'm parched.'

The pub was dark, warm and inviting. Hurricane lamps and candles lent a cosy glow to the otherwise shabby surroundings. Despite the power cuts, the mood remained upbeat, if a little subdued. Punters spoke quietly, the occasional burst of laughter bounced off the walls, the clink of glasses replaced the tinkle of the ivories.

'I like it like this,' said Florence. 'It's quite serene, like a church.'

'My kind of church!' said Stan, as he supped his pint. 'Got any confessions?'

'Oh, Stanley, that's so irreverent! You are a one!'

'Anyway, that's me done now, at the yard. Have to watch the pennies till I get some work. Must see that fella, said he could use me.'

'In the meantime, you must continue with your ideas, think furniture, Stanley!'

'I do. Gawd knows I do, but there's so much to think about, get a bit muddled sometimes. S'pose I need to draw them up properly next, exact like, and make a sample or two.'

'That's the ticket! Don't lose momentum, keep going.'

'Speaking of which,' said Stan coyly, 'we should get going, out like, you and me, have a day out together. What do you say?'

She grabbed his hands and squeezed them tight. Her face beamed like an eight year old at a birthday party.

'Oh, that's such a sweet idea! I know, how about the seaside? Be quite bracing this time of year. Lungful of salty air do us both the power of good, be just the tonic!'

'Done. We could take the train, Clacton maybe?'

'Capital! Oh, it will be nice to get away from those tykes, even if it is for just one day. I love them dearly, but there's only so much one can take from forty screaming children.'

'That's that then. Now, let's get you home so you can dream about jellied eels and ice cream.'

* * *

Stan was up at dawn. He cleared the table, sharpened his pencil and set about drawing an accurate rendition of the 'Wilkin's Recliner', which didn't recline. He moved from table to kitchen, teapot to chair, window to ashtray. By lunch he'd accomplished nothing. His mind was addled.

'I can't do it like this,' he muttered, 'I need to make the blinkin' thing, I need to make it.'

He toyed with The Overalls' card, grabbed his coat and headed for Rotherhithe.

As the Luftwaffe's target of choice, the docks had taken a pounding during the Blitz. Where once the Empire had greeted the world, stood the remnants of bombed-out buildings, ravaged by fire, hollow and bare. Stan stood awhile to take it in. No more, the smell of coffee and fruit.

No more, the smell of coal-fired tugs chugging along the Thames, just the smell of destruction, not even a whiff of renewal.

Stan found The Overalls behind the desk of a small, first floor office next door to The Jolly Waterman. He wore a tight-fitting, black suit and small bowler hat. The timbers creaked as he entered unannounced.

'Stan, what a pleasant surprise!'

'Alright?'

'I'd offer you a chair, but as you can see…'

'S'alright. Hope you don't mind me just turning up, but you did say…'

The Overalls grinned and stood to shake his hand.

'Of course not, glad you came.'

Stan shook his hand, walked over to the window and looked down at the Thames. A murky, grey Thames which seemed somehow reluctant to ebb and flow, as though it, too, had given up the ghost.

'Bleak, ain't it?' said Stan. 'Never realised it was this bad, but then again, don't really come up this way, me.'

The Overalls joined him.

'Bleak it is, but not without hope. It's an opportunity Stan, an opportunity to rebuild, re-invigorate, renew!'

'You sound like a politician! No offence, like.'

The Overalls patted him on the shoulder.

'None taken.'

'Take years, won't it?' asked Stan.

'Maybe, but the quicker we work, the sooner it will happen. Now, lot going on, I've got a role for you in mind, a sort of foreman, that suit?'

'Foreman?' said Stan, surprised. 'Well, yeah, but me?'

'Tidy mind, Stan, tidy mind. You'll do fine. Now, you'll be just over there, Greenland Dock. Start Monday, meet me here and we'll walk over, okay by you?'

'Smashing. Ta very much.'

He couldn't wait to tell Flo. Not just a job, but a foreman. Things were on the up. With that kind of money he would soon have enough to start a business, a small, one-man business, but a business all the same. The Jolly Waterman furnished him with a pint of Best by way of celebration.

* * *

Fastidious, organised, a creature of habit who enjoyed routine. That was Florence Chadwick. That's what unsettled Stan. The house was in darkness, the curtains open. A single pint of milk sat on the doorstep. He knocked for half an hour but there was no answer. She obviously wasn't home. It rankled him. Something was wrong. He told himself not to be so daft, so possessive. There was nothing to worry about. Besides, it was only seven-thirty and he wasn't her keeper. 'Bloody women,' he mumbled under his breath and returned home with a bottle of stout. He supped by the fire with Yeats on his lap:

Here we will moor our lonely ship
And wander ever with woven hands,
Murmuring softly lip to lip,
Along the grass, along the sands,
Murmuring how far away are the unquiet lands.

He thought of her neck. Her slender, elegant neck. A neck so smooth, so soft, so vulnerable. It didn't tense. It didn't flinch. It relented, as if it welcomed the touch. The touch of steel as cold as the night, as silent as the streets. One swift slice and it was done. No time to scream. No voice to be heard. Just a muted gurgle as she choked on her own blood.

* * *

Now there were two. Two pints on the doorstep. Two pints too many. Stan raced over to the school. They'd not seen Florence either, something that was so out of character they'd already contacted the police. He went back to Henshaw Street and waited. Half a packet of fags and a whole hour later, two bobbies, locked in conversation, wandered lethargically down the street.

'Oi!' yelled Stan. 'Get a move on! She could be dying in there!'

'Now then, sir,' said the older of the two, 'best calm down, ay? Let us handle this.'

He ambled up to the door, politely tapped the knocker and stood back.

'What you doing?' asked Stan.

'Knocking, sir. See if anyone's in.'

'Are you as stupid as you look?' he yelled, 'You think I haven't done that a hundred times already? Knock the bloody door down!'

The copper looked at his colleague and beckoned him forward.

'Give it a shove, lad.'

He winced as his shoulder crumpled against the door. Incensed, Stan pushed him aside, smashed his elbow through the light, reached in and turned the lock.

'You'll be liable for that, sir.'

Stan flew up the stairs calling for Flo. There was no answer. Flustered, he went back down.

'Well, well, well. Fancy seeing you here, Mr Wilkins.'

'Porter! What the bleedin' hell do you want?'

Porter smiled and spoke to his colleagues.

'Gentlemen, this is Mr Wilkins, quite a lady's man, so he is.'

'You what?' said Stan, fists clenched.

'Search this place from top to bottom, see what you can find. And stick the kettle on.'

He turned to Stan.

'Go home, Mr Wilkins. Rest assured, we'll be in touch as soon as we have anything to report.'

Porter laughed as he stormed off down the street.

* * *

Stan polished off the rest of his fags, wore a hole in the carpet and was about to hit the Scotch when there was a knock at the door. It was way past five, dark and bitterly cold.

'You best come with us,' said Porter. 'Won't take long.'

'What? You found her? Where is she? She…'

Porter held up his hand and smiled a cocky, annoying smile.

'You'll see.'

They got in the back of the police car and drove towards Flo's house.

'Hang on, this ain't her street, she's the next one up, where we going?'

'We're here. Come on,' said Porter.

He walked up to number thirty-three, sat on the wall and took out his torch.

'Recognise this?' he smirked, as he directed the beam towards the ground.

'This had better be good,' snarled Stan, 'or so help me, I'll…'

He leant over the wall. Florence stared back. Tiny, arctic white crystals of frost flecked her face. She twinkled in the torchlight like a snow fairy, her eyes wide, frozen in disbelief. He started to shake, spun to the kerb and retched. Porter chuckled.

'Something you ate?' he said.

Stan wiped his mouth, walked calmly back to the wall and sent Porter flying with a right hook that almost broke his fingers. He looked down at Flo, at her crusty scarf of crimson blood, leant forward and closed her eyes. His tears fell to her cheeks. 'You must be cold,' he whispered, as he traced a line down her nose with his index finger.

Porter stood, glaring, flanked by two constables.

'Wilkins, you're coming with us,' he said, rubbing his cheek.

'Bugger off,' said Stan. 'Bugger off and leave us alone.'

'Can't do that You've got some explaining to do.'

Stan turned around.

'Ex…? What the bleedin' hell you on about, copper?'

Porter held aloft a piece of paper. It was Stan's paypacket.

'We found this next to the body. I'm arresting you on suspicion of murder. Let's go.'

Chapter Nine

He sat, motionless, frozen by the cold, numbed by the pain. The cell was dark, as black as pitch, a morbid canvas with flashing images of Florence's face. He felt sick to the pit of his stomach and whimpered as he fought back the tears. Footsteps echoed in the corridor. A constable arrived and unlocked the door.

'Come with me,' he said.

The table was small, carved with inscriptions, tainted with confessions. He sat across from Porter. The bruise on his cheek seemed to pulse in the lamplight.

'So. Let's not beat around the bush,' he said, 'where were you last night?'

Stan raised his eyes and squinted through the gloom.

'Home.'

'All night?'

'All night.'

'Doing what?'

'Reading.'

'Reading what?'

'Poetry.'

'You what?'

'You heard.'

Porter chuckled, sat back in his chair and tapped his pencil on the table. 'Okay, okay, in that case,' he continued, 'you won't have any difficulty recalling what poems you read. Heh, go on then.'

Stan's voice was monotonously quiet.

'The Wanderings of Oisin. William Butler Yeats. Specifically, 'The Indian to His Love' and 'The Ballad of Moll Magee'.'

'Moll Magee, eh? Not Biffo the Bear? Can you prove it?'

'It's on the table. The book. Next to a bottle of Best. Empty.'

'Hmmm. Okey dokey. And before that?'

'Rotherhithe.'

'Go on.'

'Went to see a man about a dog.'

'Breed?'

'Job. Man about a job.'

'Where?'

'Greenland Docks. Start next week.'

'You'll be lucky. Here.'

Porter pushed the notepad and pencil toward Stan.

'Name and address of the bloke you saw in Rotherhithe. Got a house key? Wouldn't want to break the door down now, would we? Shouldn't take long.'

* * *

Porter sent two coppers over to Rotherhithe and took a constable with him to Stan's house who stood guard over the front door while he searched inside. He was back in a thrice.

'Nothing here,' he said, 'Let's go.'

Back at the station Porter frenetically scribbled out his report, giggling like a schoolboy. The inspector breezed by.

'Busy?' he asked.

'Chadwick case, sir,' said Porter. 'Think I've got it stitched up.'

'It's a murder inquiry, Porter, don't you think you should leave it to the detectives?'

'Yessir. No sir. Nothing to investigate, sir. Open and shut case. Just going to have another word with the suspect before charging him.'

'Is that so? Very well, I'll sit in. Come on.'

Porter hastily shuffled his papers, left them on the desk and barked at a constable to fetch Stan. He cleared his throat, glanced at the inspector and addressed Stan in the most officious tone he could muster.

'It appears the chap in Rotherhithe verified your story. In fact, he had a lot of good things to say about you.'

'No reason otherwise,' droned Stan.

'Not sure how he feels about you now, mind, but no matter. Unfortunately, however, there's no-one who can testify as to your whereabouts last night.'

'I told you, I was home. Reading.'

'Indeed you did. Alas, there was no book. Just half a dozen empty beer bottles. Funny how booze can make you, shall we say, forget?'

Stan stared at Porter. His eyes narrowed.

'I ain't forgotten nothing,' he said. 'There was one empty bottle and the book. I read and went to bed.'

'Not so. We'll do another search in the morning, a more thorough one. In the meantime…' he glanced at the inspector. 'Stanley Wilkins, I am formally…'

The inspector butted in.

'This all in your report, Porter?' he asked. 'Sorry, Mr Wilkins, this is a serious charge, I'd just like to check everything's in order.'

'Yes sir,' said Porter, 'all in my report, every last detail.'

'Good, wait here, I'll fetch it.'

The inspector left the room, Porter leaned across the table and whispered.

'Like I said, Wilkins, you'll get what's coming. Justice, fair and square. Probably a rope around your neck, too.'

Stan said nothing. The inspector returned.

'Right,' he said, opening a manila file, 'I'll just have a flick through this. Assume this is yours, Porter, trying to better yourself, are you?'

He tossed the copy of *Oisin* on to the table. It landed with a thud. Stan's eyes drifted slowly from the book to meet Porter's. His face twitched. He sat back in his chair, cracked his knuckles and turned to the inspector.

'I wish to make a complaint,' said Stan. 'A very formal complaint.'

* * *

He was home before sunrise. He sat, suffocated by sorrow in the stale, stagnant air of the dining room. Head hung low, he pulled *Oisin* from his pocket and laid it on the table. He counted the bottles. One. One empty bottle. One solitary, empty bottle. The words whirled around his head, 'half a dozen empty beer bottles, half a dozen empty beer bottles'. His eyes widened, he clenched his teeth, grabbed the bottle and smashed it against the table,

'Bastard!' he yelled, 'Bastard!'. He stabbed the table with the neck of the bottle till he could hold it no more. His hand dripped with blood, lacerated by the shards. He fell back to the chair and sobbed until he slept.

* * *

Florence hee-hawed as she took his arm. Her coppery locks glistened in the low, winter sun. He felt her hand in his and kissed her gently on the lips. She was sitting on the window seat, in the bay, sewing, with a gin and tonic by her side. He listened as she enthused about The Wilkins Recliner and smiled. The train rattled as it bounced, side to side, clickity-clacking to Clacton. He lowered the window and leaned out. A blast of cold, salty air blew life into his lungs. Florence pulled him back and berated him for being so childish. They laughed and hugged. He took her face in his hands and kissed her on the forehead. Such a pretty face, such a perfect face, flecked with frost, frozen in fear, eyes like pools of despair. The knock at the door woke him with a start.

'Sorry to bother you, Mr Wilkins,' said the inspector, 'mind if I come in?'

Stan stood aside and ushered him into the living room.

'Just woke up,' said Stan. 'Bit of a night.'

The inspector sighed.

'Yes. I know,' he said. 'I won't keep you long. First of all, I'd like to apologise, again, for the way this inquiry has been handled. Sergeant Porter, as you are well aware, overstepped the mark. He will be disciplined, severely, mark my words, and if you want to bring a charge of false arrest, harassment, etcetera, I won't stand in your way. In fact, I'll back you up.'

‘Thanks,’ said Stan. ‘I’ll think about it. No, no, it’s stupid. Maybe. Let’s just leave it, eh? Got enough to worry about, right now.’

‘Of course,’ said the inspector. 'I understand. Last point, the funeral. It will be a week today, Camberwell New Cemetery, I’ll let you know the precise time in a day or two.’

‘Right you are,’ said Stan. ‘One thing. Headstone. I’d like to take care of that, if that’s alright?’

‘Course, sir. No problem. If you pop by the station, they’ll let you know who to see about it.’

‘Ta. Ta, very much.’

* * *

Stan wallowed in the bath and tried to scrub the memories from his mind, Porter’s malicious interpretation of justice, the clammy claustrophobia of clink and Flo’s frozen façade, but they were indelible. He lay back till the water lapped his ears, further still till it bathed his eyes, then he took a breath and slipped under. The bubbles bobbed to the surface, slowly, a few at a time. He opened his mouth. He couldn’t swallow. He couldn’t breathe. He couldn’t do it. Coughing and gasping, he wrenched himself from the tub and collapsed on the floor, calling for Flo.

* * *

‘We’re just about to close, sir, but if it’s about your loss, do come in.’

It was a sombre place, Albin’s. Deathly quiet. A faint trace of lavender hung in the air. The funeral director gave a reassuring but subtle smile, tilted his head and spoke softly.

‘How may I help?’

'Erm, headstone,' said Stan. 'It's about the headstone for me, you know, the coppers, they told to come here.'

'Of course. May I have the name?'

'Stanley Wilkins. She's Flo. Florence Chadwick.'

The undertaker drew a sharp breath. Stan was surprised, and touched, he looked genuinely upset.

'Such a tragic affair,' he said, 'I am truly sorry.'

'Ta,' said Stan. 'Much appreciated. I, er, I brought this. This is what I'd like on the wotsit. After her name, if that's alright.'

He handed him a piece of paper covered with another example of his finest hand.

For she comes, the human child
To the waters and the wild
With a faery, hand in hand
From a world more full of weeping
Than she can understand

The undertaker smiled and nodded.

'Yeats,' he said. 'Beautiful.'

* * *

Bills. Bills were the only letters to ever grace his doormat. He trod on it as he stepped indoors. Right colour envelope, wrong shape. Intrigued, he ripped it open instead of shoving it with the others behind the clock on the mantlepiece. It was from the council. It was time for the developers to move in. Time to rebuild the street so folk could return home. His home was the only one standing. His home was the only obstruction. It was a simple, no-nonsense offer written in a matter-of-fact way. £300.00 and off you go, take it or leave it. Leave it and we'll force you to go, without the £300.00. 'Three hundred quid?' sighed Stan. 'Time to move on.'

The Overalls offered Stan time off to attend the funeral, time off to make arrangements, time off to grieve. Stan declined. He didn't go to the funeral. Nor did he ever see the headstone. 'She's right here,' he said, tapping the side of his head with his forefinger, 'always will be.' He did, however, accept the offer of a day off to move, as soon as he found somewhere suitable, that was. 'Suitable' was a ten minute walk from the docks, suitable was private, suitable was 66 Lower Road. He rented it and moved, lock, stock and barrel, in a single morning. He spent the afternoon in The Cock o' Monkey and returned home late, plastered.

* * *

Porter was deskbound, duties curtailed. Filing did not bring out his natural enthusiasm for convicting criminals. He sifted through the large, cardboard box marked 'Lost Property' under orders to discard anything more than twelve months old, unless it was valuable, in which case such items would be sold off, proceeds going towards the Police Benevolent Fund. Dentures, upper set, he deemed worthless. House keys, useless without a lock. Wallet, leather, empty, was saleable. As was the walking cane and wristwatch. The ring also had a value. Gold. He felt a chill run down his spine as he read the inscription. He held it to his lips as he pondered the obvious question: 'If she had done a flit to Margate, why would she leave her ring behind? Widower or not, women were not in the habit of discarding jewellery. And how come it was found in Llewellyn's yard?' He glanced over his shoulder and popped the ring in his pocket. 'Knew it,' he muttered. 'I bloody well knew it.'

Porter removed his helmet, stood back and scratched his head. Where once stood the house belonging to Stanley Wilkins lay a pile of rubble. He swore under his breath, clueless as to his whereabouts. Then he remembered. The docks. Greenland docks. His shift finished at four. He went home, changed into civvies, and hurried over. He was just in time to see them knocking off. He watched as Stan waved to his workmates, close enough to hear him decline the offer of a pint in the Watermen. He waited and followed. Stan did not go home. He went to The Mayflower instead. He stood at the back of the pub, pint in hand and stared out across the Thames. He'd almost supped the last when he felt a presence behind him. He turned to see Porter. Porter reached inside his pocket and brought out the ring. He held it, shoulder high, betwixt his thumb and forefinger. His gaze did not waver. Stan recognised it instantly but said nothing. He drained his glass and left. Porter cackled aloud, knocked back his pint and followed Stan into the night. It was drizzling and cold. The cobbles glistened in the moonlight. There was not a soul to be seen, not a sound to be heard. He turned up his collar and began walking. Stan was nowhere to be seen. The blow to the back of his head knocked him out. He fell, face down. Stan dropped the pipe, it clanged as it rolled to the kerb. He stood, he watched, he listened. No-one came. He reached down and took the ring from Porter's pocket. He was tempted to relieve him of his wallet too, so it would like a robbery, but a thief, he was not.

Chapter Ten

A year had taken its toll. Stan's was a world of melancholy mundaneness, his demeanour was dour, his hair, grey and thinning. He'd given up on the pubs, the merry Mayflower and the convivial Cock o' Monkey. Times had changed, folk had become insular and selfish, and so he kept himself to himself, preferring instead the impersonal service of the off-licence and the comfort of his armchair to a tavern full of transients. He knew what people thought, he saw the way they looked at him, 'the old bloke', 'the miserable git who never smiles', 'the loner'. But they didn't know what he knew, they hadn't lost what he'd lost, and they couldn't see the enormous weight on his shoulders which caused him to stoop like a sycophantic Dickensian beggar. The Overalls' optimistic vision of the future was taking shape, the docks were being rejuvenated, but it was time for the labourers to make way for the planners. His passion for progress crumbled with every redundancy note he wrote. Stan stood cheek to jowl with the other men and watched as he handed them out. He made it his duty to thank each and every one of them in person. He felt responsible and found it difficult to cope with the sight of hard-working, honest men on the scrap-heap with the twisted, rusted girders and the smell of coffee and bananas. Stan mustered a smile as The Overalls slapped him on the arm. 'Not all bad!' he said, 'Something good will come of this. Must have a pint someday, eh?' Stan nodded and wished him well. He knew that would never happen.

* * *

Second post arrived. He shuffled to the door and groaned as he picked up the pile of manilla. Gas. Electric. Rates, final demand. The Post Office Savings Book was dog-eared and worn. He scanned the entries, not a single deposit since the cheque he got for the house, just line after line of withdrawals. He counted out his severance pay and added it all together. At best, he had a year. In reality, probably more like six months. He made a mental note to go see the council about a flat. He was getting on, almost retired and unemployable, not that there were any jobs to be had anyway. The last envelope, by contrast, was white. Pure, unsullied white, with an odd franking mark in the top right hand corner. It was from the cops. They'd given up. After years of enquiries they'd got nowhere, no evidence, no proof, no convictions nor suspicions. The file was taking up space on the shelf. Sincere apologies but so far as Florence Chadwick was concerned, it was case closed. Murder. Unsolved. He considered going to the cemetery, then had an even better idea. It said 'Teacher's' on the label. How appropriate, he thought. 'No proof. I've got 40% proof. Cheers.' He settled into his armchair and slowly fell into a stupor fuelled by barley and water.

* * *

'Brand new! You'll be one of the first,' enthused the housing officer. His hair dripped with the contents of a deep fat fryer and his aftershave reeked of misanthropy and greed. He puffed on a fag and grinned like a half-wit. Stan regarded him with contempt.

'How'd you get a job 'ere?' he asked.

'Good looks and charm,' came the reply.

Stan sighed.

'Gawd help us,' he said. 'Alright, what is it? Where you putting me?'

'Up the road from where you are now, fifteen-minute walk. Two beds, lounge, kitchen, bathroom…'

'Garden?'

'Er, no. No garden.'

'Not far, you say?'

'Not far at all.'

'Alright, let's take a gander.'

* * *

They stopped short of the docks. The apathetic greaseball kept his hands in his pockets and nodded towards the housing development.

'Here we are,' he said, 'the Zanzibar estate.'

Stan squinted through the drizzle. He could see rows of small, modern, terraced houses with tiny, courtyard gardens, arranged in neat blocks of ten. There was a large, green area with newly planted trees and shrubs, and there were two gargantuan high-rise buildings, sixteen floors tall, rising like concrete carbuncles from the dust and the rubble. He'd never seen anything like it. Worse still, he hadn't even noticed them going up.

Stan turned to the housing officer and spoke quietly.

'This look like Zanzibar to you?' he griped.

'Dunno. Never been. Anyway, they called it after the docks, over there, you know, Zanzibar Docks.'

'You astound me.'

They clambered across the debris towards the carbuncles. Stan stopped in his tracks, wiped the rain from his nose and yelled at his guide.

'Oi! Where we goin'?'

'Up there.'

'I can't live up there. Why can't I have one of them?' he asked, pointing to the terraces.

'All gone.'

'Well, how the bleedin' hell am I gonna get up there?'

'Technology.'

'Twit.'

They took the lift to the fourteenth floor. Stan held the wall for support as he stepped out. He didn't like technology. He didn't like change. 'This ain't natural,' he muttered, 'If we was meant to be this high, we'd live in nests.'

'Blimey! That the river? Never seen it from above,' he said.

'Not many people have, Mr Wilkins. If you look out the bedroom, you can see the docks.'

'I dunno. Don't feel right somehow. Ain't ya got something a bit, you know, a bit lower? Bit nearer the ground, like? Don't I get a choice?'

'Yeah, course you do. Hobson's.'

'Bleedin' comedian, eh? Who's gonna get me stuff?'

* * *

Stan spent the entire day gazing from his lofty perch. He watched the Thames flow by below him, followed the tugs as they chugged upstream and swore at the pigeons on the balcony. 'Bloody marvellous,' he sighed as the sun set slowly behind St. Paul's. He hadn't unpacked. Nor washed. Nor eaten. But he was thirsty. The lift arrived and the doors glided silently apart. He smiled, gingerly stepped inside and stabbed '0' with his forefinger. A group of kids kicked a battered football around the green. He heard a baby screaming for its mother. A young couple strolled arm in arm toward the terraces. 'S'alright this,' he thought.

He sat back with a glass of ale and pulled the watch from his pocket. 'Bloody Nora!' he exclaimed. It had taken him almost an hour to get to the off-licence and back. 'This won't do. Won't do at all.'

* * *

The following morning he unpacked what few possessions he had and whistled contentedly as he found them all a home – clothes: wardrobe, pictures: sideboard, medals: mantlepiece, crockery: kitchen, and tools: cupboard. He soaked in the tub and admired the pristine white tiles while his toes wrinkled like dried prunes. Dapper in a clean shirt and tie, he ventured out to stock up on essentials. Two hours later he returned, laden with groceries and arms two inches longer than he remembered them being. He had enough food and beer for three days, and for three days he stayed put, watching and listening, but heard nothing, not even a neighbour. When the food ran out he had no option but to do the same. It was already getting tiresome. He returned with another load, pushed the button on the lift, and waited. And waited. And waited. A respectable-looking woman emerged from the stairwell. She was smartly dressed and about the same age as himself. She greeted him politely and advised him to take a seat on the steps.

'Not working love,' she said, 'bust already. Could be ages before the bloke turns up to fix it.'

Stan looked to the heavens.

'Bleedin' technology! How am I supposed to get up there, then?'

'Up where?' she asked.

'Fourteenth floor. Where the pigeons live.'

She chuckled and touched his arm.

'Oh, you are funny. Look, if it ain't done by the time I get back, I shan't be long, you can come sit with me, I'm only one floor up.'

'Much obliged,' said Stan, 'much obliged indeed. Stan's the name. Stanley Wilkins.'

'Margaret, but everyone calls me Marge. See ya.'

* * *

Unfortunately, the engineer arrived before Margaret returned. He fiddled around in the box behind the buttons and insisted on going with Stan all the way to the top, just to be sure everything was working, as it should be. They stopped at every floor along the way. At every floor he sighed, stepped out into the lobby, sighed, and stepped back in again. Fifteen minutes passed before they reached the eighth floor.

'For Gawd's sake! Can't you do this on the bleedin' way down?' griped Stan.

The engineer eyed him with contempt.

'If you don't like it, you can always walk,' he said.

* * *

Stan stood by the window and stared at his reflection. Save for the handful of lights dotted along the embankment, little else could be seen. The wireless crackled as it struggled to lock-on to a signal. He went to the door and listened for signs of life in the hallway. The flat was cold. He turned on the heat. Modern, electric heat at the flick of a switch. No open fires, no chimneys, no smell of coal, no warmth, no real warmth, nothing tangible to feel or behold. He couldn't hear the blackbirds, though he knew they were there, somewhere. He couldn't see the street or the strays that patrolled it. He yearned to look at trees instead of clouds and people instead of his own, sorry face. He felt the walls closing in, he was cut-off, detached, isolated and depressed. He opened a beer, pulled Yeats from the box of odds and sods, and began to read.

She bid me take life easy, as the grass grows on the weirs;
But I was young and foolish, and now am full of tears.

'That's all I bleedin' need.' He sighed, and shut the book. He rummaged through the box. Pencils, a candle, box of matches, a sign which read 'Office', a six inch rule, two barley sugars and a wedge of papers, creased and worn. He pulled them to his lap, lit a fag and sifted through them. A bill. Another bill. Then a sketch. An accomplished sketch of a chair. 'The Wilkins Recliner'. He searched for the others, regarded them with a nostalgic fondness, then ripped them to shreds. Every last one. He sat back and fell asleep as he reminisced about Flo.

* * *

'I remembered,' she said. 'I remembered you said you lived with the pigeons, so I thought I'd come see how you're settling in. Bought us a bit of cake.'

Stan was elated.

'Blimey! Margaret, ain't it? This is a welcome surprise. Don't stand there, come in, come in. Welcome to my ivory tower!'

Margaret smiled, wiped her feet on the mat and strode down the hall.

'Oh, don't you get a lovely view from up 'ere,' she said.

'You're welcome to it. Nothing changes up 'ere. Not a bleedin' thing. Novelty soon wears off. 'Ere, give us your coat, take a pew. I'll stick the kettle on.'

Margaret sat at the table and pondered the view upstream.

'I don't see this down there,' she said. 'Just walls and houses. Everything's grey. Bit noisy too, mind.'

'Swap.'

She laughed.

'Not on your Nellie. Like my feet on the ground. Ta, but no ta.'

'Sugar? Or you sweet enough?'

'You cheeky sod! Have to watch you, won't I? Two please. Heaped.'

* * *

Margaret enjoyed visiting Stan and he was grateful of the company. It began with the occasional pot of tea and a couple of biscuits. He liked it like that, it made living in the clouds just about bearable. He got to talk with someone, socialise a bit, but on the whole, still kept himself to himself. If there was one thing he couldn't abide, it was nosey neighbours. The occasional pot of tea turned into something more regular, three times a week, then four, then five. Then the tea turned into lunch, and lunch into dinner. She would arrive with a pot of steaming stew or a plate of chops before laying claim to his kitchen and taking sole command of his domestic habits. Her heart was in the right place but her kindness was too intrusive. He felt smothered and took to ignoring the knocks at the door. 'Meddling Marge' was getting on his wick.

'At last!' she said. 'Been worried sick about you, I have! Where you been?'

'Nowhere. Don't go nowhere, me. What you want?'

'Grub! Made it yesterday, we can just heat it up.'

'Not hungry, ta all the same.'

'Got to keep your strength up, Stan, come on, stick it on the stove.'

'I said, I'm not... oh what's the bleedin' use, come on, get yourself inside.'

'That's more like it,' she said, and plonked the pan on the counter.

She turned to Stan and grinned.

'Straighten your tie, Stan, it's all crooked. Look at you, don't you shave no more? 'Ere, I had a thought, you never come see me, got a nice place I have. Why don't ya come to mine for a change?'

'Legs. Trouble with the legs. Can't go far. Shrapnel I expect.'

'But you only have to get in the lift.'

'It's only the lift to you. It's a bloomin' mile for me.'

'Oh. Alright then.'

She put the pan on the stove and filled the kettle.

'You could always stop over,' she said. 'Plenty of room.'

Stan said nothing. She forced a smile and cleared her throat.

'Tell ya what, you sit down, love, I'll take care of this.'

'As usual.'

'Where's the teapot? Always warm the pot first, remember that.'

'Remember that,' he muttered.

'I'll just give the floor a quick sweep, bit dusty ain't it? Won't take a mo'.'

'Won't take a mo'.'

'Saw a lovely looking frock this morning, down the market, expect you was still in bed. Didn't have me size, though. Not to worry, got plenty of frocks. Still, nice to look one's best, ain't it?'

'Ain't it.'

'Speaking of which, look at your shirt! Needs a good soak, that does. I'll do it tomorrow.'

Stan stared out the window, head in hands. He massaged his grey temples and lit a fag.

'Oh Stan, we're just about to eat, you can put that out now.'

'Put that out now. Put that out now! Stop it! Shut ya bleedin' gob, for Chrissakes woman! Shut it!'

Margaret froze. Stunned by his outburst. The words bounced off her armour-plated skin. She wasn't scared, nor was she frightened. She was offended. Deeply offended.

'Well, I never! Never heard the likes of it!'

Stan swivelled in his seat to face her.

'Listen,' he began, 'I know you mean well, but you're meddlin', meddlin' in me life. Leave off.'

She wiped her hands furiously on a tea towel and sat opposite him.

'Only trying to help,' she said. 'Just being neighbourly. Thought you wanted company.'

'No! You want company, not me.'

'Well, if that's the way you feel…'

'It is.'

'I'll just clean up, then I'll be on me way.'

'There ya go again, see!'

'What?'

'Cleaning! Leave it!'

His neck twitched. He could feel his heart pounding against his ribs. He looked across the table and saw his mother.

'I think you should go,' he said, stood up and went to kitchen.

Margaret spoke softly.

'It's just a tiff, Stan. Everyone has a spat now and then.'

Stan stood behind her. His knuckles turned white as he gripped the carving knife.

'You don't get it, do ya? I mean, I think you should go.'

Chapter Eleven

Porter enjoyed his retirement. He enjoyed pottering around his allotment, sharing his shallow expertise on crop-rotation and advising the uninitiated on the best method of growing runner beans. He enjoyed watching Columbo on his brand-new television set while he ate his supper. And he enjoyed reading the newspaper from cover to cover, particularly when a villain had been caught and sent down for a substantial term, particularly when it mentioned someone he knew, particularly when it made the hairs stand on the back of his neck.

He read with intrigue of a nurse who had gone missing in Bermondsey a fortnight earlier. She was responsible, affable and well-respected in the community. Her disappearance, it seemed, was completely out of character. The last known person to have seen her was Mrs Edna Williams of Albion Street, who was receiving treatment for a swollen ankle. According to her, Nurse Mary O'Shaughnessy left in good spirits, keen to clear her last appointment of the day with a Mr Stanley Wilkins

Porter slapped the table with his hand and sat, open-mouthed, as his brain clicked into gear. 'Nurse goes missing. Stanley Wilkins. Nah, surely not. Surely he's dead by now.' He closed the paper, made himself a brew and settled into his armchair. Something niggled him. It was too much of a coincidence. How many Stanley Wilkins could there be? He went back to the paper and re-read the article. A sadistic grin crept across his face. 'You never know, I think it's time we re-opened the case of Miss Eileen Doyle,' he muttered, 'and one or two others.'

He went to his study and scanned the bookcase where everything was meticulously arranged in alphabetical order. He traced a finger along the row of neatly labelled files on the top shelf: 'Allotment', 'Deeds', 'Electricity Bills', 'Gas Bills', 'Insurance Policies', 'Life Assurance', 'Missing Persons'.

'Ahh! Missing Persons!' he whispered, 'gone, but not forgotten.'

He sat at his desk and removed decades worth of newspaper clippings till he found what he was looking for: his notebooks, paperwork and charge sheets. 'Now then, let's get to work.' He was surprised at how vivid his recollections were as he read through his notes and went back to his days as an eager young copper, keen to please, desperate to convict. He could picture Stan in his mind's eye, his rakish good looks, his battle-scarred face, and slowly realised the driving force behind his passion to nail him had been jealousy. After all, Stan had been to foreign lands, he'd taught himself a trade or two, he was confident and capable of looking after himself and he never had any trouble finding female companions. Female companions, the one thing Porter had never enjoyed. He began to hate him all over again. He snapped his pencil, gathered up his paperwork and went to bed.

* * *

'Yes sir, the person you want to see is D.I. Hanlon. I'll see if he's available.'

Porter waited patiently by the counter, briefcase in one hand, warrant card in the other. Hanlon appeared and regarded him quizzically.

'You wanted to see me?' he asked.

'Indeed,' said Porter. 'Indeed. The Mary O'Shaughnessy case. I believe I have something you may be interested in.'

He proffered his old warrant card.

'Retired now, of course,' he said.

'Follow me.'

Hanlon led him to his office, closed the blinds and offered him a seat.

'So,' he said, 'what you got?'

He listened attentively as Porter droned on about his endeavours to prosecute Wilkins but how a lack of evidence prevented him from securing a conviction. 'Know how frustrating that is, when you know someone done it, but you can't nab 'em?' He battered Hanlon's ears for more than four hours with all the facts and circumstances surrounding the disappearance of Eileen Doyle, Gladys Wilkins and Jean Partridge. Hanlon made occasional notes on a pad, doodled more frequently and eventually yawned in such a way that Porter got the hint. He took a sip of water and sat back.

'So. What d'ya think?' he asked. 'Think he's worth pursuing?'

Hanlon perked up and feigned enthusiasm out of respect for the old-timer.

'It's all very interesting, Mr Porter,' he said 'very interesting indeed, but you see, the problem I have here is that this is all circumstantial, there isn't a shred of hard evidence. Unless we can secure a confession, or positively link him to the disappearance of Mary O'Shaughnessy, we haven't a hope in hell of bringing this to trial. That is, of course, assuming we're both talking about the same Stanley Wilkins.'

'Trust me, there is only one Stanley Wilkins, and you have to admit, it's all a bit close to the bone ain't it? Bit much to be a coincidence.'

Hanlon sighed and had to admit he had a point.

'Alright, Mr Porter, I'll give you that, it does look as though it's more than just coincidence, but as I've already said, everything you've told me will only hold water if we can prove he was responsible for O'Shaughnessy's disappearance. That is the only link we have.'

'Then bloody well use it! You seen him yet, Wilkins? You questioned him, been round his gaff?'

'Not yet. Tomorrow maybe. Day after perhaps.'

'I'd like to come along,' said Porter, already twitching in his seat, 'I think I could be useful, might be able to help jog his mind if need be.'

'I'm not sure,' said Hanlon, 'you're not officially on the case and…'

'As an observer then. Look, we both know coppers need help, wherever it comes from,' he stabbed the air with his finger, 'and you need my help.'

Hanlon felt he should reprimand Porter for his outburst, his forthright manner, but couldn't bring himself to do it.

'Way you're carrying on,' he said, 'anyone would think it's you with something to hide.'

Porter laughed. Nervously.

'Alright. Give me your number. I'll ring and let you know.'

* * *

It was dark. A fine drizzle blew gently round the tower block. They parked by the entrance. A group of teenagers huddled against the wall and watched their every move. Hanlon helped Porter from the car.

'Blimey,' said Porter. 'What a dump. Better lock it or it won't be 'ere when we get back.'

'Go wait by the door, out of the rain,' said Hanlon. 'Be with you in minute.'

A squad car arrived and pulled up alongside. Two uniform and a lady got out, exchanged words with Hanlon and made their way towards Porter.

'Mr Porter, this is D.S. Scott,' said Hanlon. 'She's on the case.'

'Dear, oh, dear,' sighed Porter. 'Woman detective? Whatever next?'

The uniformed constables took one lift, Hanlon, Scott and Porter rode the other. It stank of cigarettes and urine. Hanlon covered his finger with his cuff and pushed the button for the fourteenth floor. It clunked to a halt and the doors stuttered as they opened. Hanlon turned to the other two and spoke quietly.

'This is a gentle line of enquiry, not a witch hunt Porter, remember that.'

He rapped the door with his knuckles.

'D.I. Hanlon,' he said. 'Walworth C.I.D. This is D.C. Porter, retired, and Detective Sergeant Scott. We're looking for Stanley Wilkins.'

They made their way down the hall to the living room. Stan was seated at the table with his back to them, sipping a glass of port. He could see their reflection in the window.

'Stanley Wilkins?'

'That you, Plod? Blimey! If it ain't Constable Porter! Don't you ever give up?'

'You know what they say, Stanley, slowly, slowly, catchey monkey.'

'That about sums you up, don't it Porter? Never made it to organ grinder, did ya?'

Hanlon stepped forward, keen to avoid a fracas.

'Mr Wilkins, this won't take long. Just a few questions if you don't mind. We're trying to trace a Miss Mary O'Shaughnessy, nurse. I understand she was treating you.'

'S'right,' said Stan. 'Exercises, for me legs. Don't work like they used to.'

'I see. Can you tell me, do you remember when you saw her last?'

'Nope. Memory's going too. Not for a while though, tell ya that for nothing.'

D.S. Scott coughed politely. She picked up the handbag on the sofa and held it aloft. Hanlon raised his eyebrows, Porter's face broke into a wide grin.

'Er, can you, can you explain the handbag, Mr Wilkins?' asked Hanlon.

'What handbag?' He turned to look at the D.S. 'Nope. Might belong to the bloke next door, dunno.'

Scott quickly rifled through the contents and pulled out a driving licence.

'Sir,' she said, 'it's hers alright.'

Hanlon sighed. He didn't want to bang up a pensioner.

'Bag it,' he said.

Reluctantly, he stepped forward and patted Stan on the shoulder.

'Sorry, Mr Wilkins, I'm afraid you'll have to come with us.'

'Come with you? Not on your bleedin' Nellie.'

'I'm afraid you don't have a choice, sir. We have evidence which leads us to believe you may have been involved with the disappearance of Mary O'Shaughnessy.'

'Listen, Plod, I told you, I ain't goin' down no…'

He was interrupted by the commotion at the door. The uniforms were remonstrating with a lady.

'I told you, miss, you can't go in there! Now kindly move awa…'

'Leave me be you damn fool!' shrilled a Galway voice. 'Don't you dare touch me, I know my rights!'

She blundered down the hall to be met by looks of surprise from Hanlon, Scott and Porter.

'What's going on here?' she screamed. 'Why are there police at the door, has something happened to the old fool?'

D.S. Scott held up the handbag.

'Is this yours, miss?' she asked.

'Oh, for the love of God, you have it. Thought I'd lost it for good.'

'Mary O'Shaughnessy?'

'That's right. Have I done something wrong?'

'No,' said Scott, 'but we would like to know where you've been for the last fortnight. You're officially a missing person you know.'

She slumped on the sofa.

'I never thought. Sweet Jesus, I've been a fool. I never thought to tell anyone, except the NHS, to arrange cover, did they not tell you I was called away?'

'No, miss,' said Hanlon. 'Not a word.'

'Feckin' useless bunch. I told them to arrange cover. I got a phone call, after I left Edna, my mammy, taken poorly, so she was. I had to leave in a hurry, me mind was all over the shop. I came and saw the old fool here, then left.'

Porter's face dropped. He eyed her with contempt. The do-gooder nurse had robbed him of his final chance. He sat quietly in the corner and said nothing. Hanlon breathed a sigh of relief.

'Well, that's that then. Sorry to have bothered you, Mr Wilkins. Hope the intrusion wasn't too unsettling.'

'S'alright, Plod. All in a day's work I s'pose. Safe 'ome.'

Hanlon handed the nurse his card.

'Miss, if you wouldn't mind dropping by tomorrow, just a formality, won't take long. Get you back in the land of the living, so to speak.'

She took the card and her bag.

'Course not,' she said. 'Hope I didn't cause too much bother. I best be off meself. Stanley Wilkins, I'll be seeing you next week, as usual.'

Stan remained seated as they filed towards the door. Porter got up and stood behind him. Stan looked at his reflection.

‘Not joining your mates, Plod? Something you forgotten?’

‘I never forget, Wilkins. Razor sharp me. Razor sharp.’

‘Mind you don’t cut yourself. You never did like me, did ya, Plod?’

‘That’s only cos I know what you done.’

‘Done? Me? You don’t know the half of it, and you’re still trying to get me.’

Porter cackled quietly and reached in his pocket.

‘Oh, I got you years ago, Wilkins, years ago. Right where it hurts.’

He pulled out a crucifix, a gold crucifix on a chain, with a topaz stone set in the centre. He dangled it in front of his face.

‘Whasat?’ said Stan as he tried to focus.

A stark look of realisation blanched his face as the crucifix dropped to the table. Porter cackled again. Stan clutched at the cross and gasped for air, his breath came in short, heavy bursts. Tears began to cloud his vision. He clutched his chest.

‘You!’ he wheezed. ‘You done it! You cut my Flo…’

Porter ambled out the door.

‘Better call an ambulance,’ he told a uniform, ‘think he’s taken a turn for the worse.’

Epilogue

The sirens didn't draw me from the flat, the noise did, the shouting and the swearing outside the front door. I figured at best it was Stan playing up, at worse, it was a bunch of scallies taunting the police officers. I went to have a look. I didn't expect to see a bunch of paramedics. And I certainly didn't expect to see Stan being stretchered into the lift with an oxygen mask clamped over his face. He was as pale as the driven snow, his eyes were shut, his brow, furrowed. I asked them what was going on. All I got was 'heart attack'. They wouldn't say anything else, wouldn't even tell me where he was going. I told them he was on his own, no next of kin, that I didn't mind staying with him. They wouldn't have it. In fact they were blunt to the point of being rude. 'Cops called us, they'll look after him.' I didn't believe it for a minute but there was little else I could do. I felt sorry for him. No-one should die alone, he should have had someone with him. I saw a crucifix wrapped around his fist. I never had him down as the religious sort but I guess he must've been. That's the thing about those tower blocks, those vertical villages, they're anything but. If you want somewhere to hide away, somewhere isolated and cold, somewhere where you can die in your bed and fester for weeks till someone remembers you, then they're perfect. It made me feel uncomfortable. I suppose Stan, in a way, was one of the lucky ones, at least he had people around him. I wondered how many others had met their maker in blissful solitude. I wondered how many people had an epitaph that read 'Went to Zanzibar and died'.

The following day I rang around the hospitals and finally found him at St. Thomas's. It was too late. He'd passed away peacefully during the night. Poor sod. His flat remained locked, the door bound in blue and white tape.

I didn't hang around much after that, a couple of weeks at most. With the passing of Stan I felt it was time to move on as well. Anyway, I was getting tired of forcing a grin and chatting politely every time Beau Brummell caught me on the landing. It was time to head somewhere new, somewhere more exciting, somewhere more 'exotic'. I packed my bags, locked the door and headed east. The mystical east. A new life, a new beginning in the land of the rising sun. The Orient. Well, Leyton to be precise. Land of chicken shops and nail bars, pound-a-pint pubs and dodgy car lots, hairdressers and bookies, and all-you-can-eat Chinese buffets.

The flat was nice, Victorian, maisonette. I liked it mainly because it was on the ground floor and didn't stink of fags and urine. I had my own front door and nice neighbours, salt-of-the-earth die hard East End neighbours who enjoyed talking, with anyone and everyone. In fact, some of them, I swear, would sit and watch from behind their net curtains till they saw someone leave their house, then they'd rush out and corner them for half an hour to natter about the amount of foreigners moving in and the lack of parking spaces. No, they weren't shy and they didn't hide away. Except the bloke who lived upstairs. He was different. Nice enough, polite enough, friendly enough, but odd. His name was Calvin. Calvin Clarke. He was Jamaican, sixty, sixty-five years old, a retired bus driver and leading light in the local gospel choir. He dressed sharp, I mean immaculate, in an 'old-fashioned suit' kind of a way. He always had a smile for everyone he knew but he rarely saw them because, apart from church, he never went out, till two o'clock in the morning that is. Then he'd return at dawn and sleep for most of the day. I wondered what he did with his time, if he was a drug dealer, a kerb crawler or simply an insomniac. Whatever he was, he had his routine, which included doing the washing at ten o'clock at night, bathing at eleven thirty then playing the piano into the small hours. Every so often, by which I mean every other week, he would return from church off a Saturday night with a friend. A lady friend, purportedly from the choir. She would stay the night, maybe two or three, then I'd never see her again. A fortnight later and another would turn up. And so it went on. I could only assume the choir comprised four hundred and twenty-two female members and one Calvin Clarke. Funny thing was, once they'd gone, he'd spend the next few nights making a right old din, hammering and sawing or something. I never slept much during those periods. I joked to myself that there was only one place his lady friends could have gone and that was under the floorboards.

He used to wash his car religiously, every Sunday, so long as it wasn't raining. It would take him a couple of hours so I'd invariably have to stop to chat on my way out. Every time he washed it he'd say the same old thing, 'Damn trees man, the blinkin' sap ruin me car!' It was a part of the neighbourly banter, something you had to hear before you could move on to another topic. One particularly fine, sunny morning we got to chatting as usual and I commented on the fine looking lass I saw leaving his flat the night before. He laughed. I called him the Jamaican Gigolo. He clicked his fingers and laughed some more. His 'ha-ha' laugh.

'What can I say, son? Me enjoy the company of women,' he said, 'make me smile, keep me young, eh! But dat's not all, me enjoy a spot of decorating too.'

If you enjoyed this book, please let others know by leaving a quick review on Amazon. Also, if you spot anything untoward in the paperback, get in touch. We strive for the best quality and appreciate reader feedback.

editor@thebookfolks.com

www.thebookfolks.com

ALSO BY PETE BRASSETT

The DI Munro & DS Charlie West Scottish murder mystery series:

SHE – book 1
AVARICE – book 2
ENMITY – book 3
DUPLICITY – book 4
TERMINUS – book 5
TALION – book 6
PERDITION – book 7

Other titles:

THE WILDER SIDE OF CHAOS
YELLOW MAN
CLAM CHOWDER AT LAFAYETTE AND SPRING
THE GIRL FROM KILKENNY
BROWN BREAD
PRAYER FOR THE DYING
KISS THE GIRLS

Made in the USA
San Bernardino, CA
28 December 2019